"YOU DO EXACTLY WHAT I SAY OR I KILL THIS BOY."

The lowlife grinned at Clint Adams, his arm around the boy's throat, holding his gun in his right hand. "Take your gun and drop it onto the floor."

"I don't think so," Adams replied.

"Do it!" the man snapped. "I'll kill this kid. I will." He screwed the barrel of his gun into the boy's ear. "Come on Adams. What's it gonna be?"

"Just give me a few seconds more."

"For what?" the man said angrily.

A voice behind the man said, "For me to blow a hole in your head."

DON'T MISS THESE
ALL-ACTION WESTERN SERIES
FROM THE BERKLEY PUBLISHING GROUP

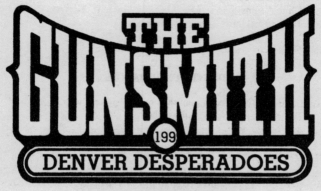

THE GUNSMITH

199

DENVER DESPERADOES

J. R. ROBERTS

DENVER DESPERADOES

A Jove Book / published by arrangement with
the author

PRINTING HISTORY
Jove edition / August 1998

The Penguin Putnam Inc. World Wide Web site address is
http://www.penguinputnam.com

ISBN: 0-515-12341-2

A JOVE BOOK®
Jove Books are published by The Berkley Publishing Group,
a member of Penguin Putnam Inc.,
200 Madison Avenue, New York, New York 10016.
JOVE and the "J" design are trademarks
belonging to Jove Publications, Inc.

PRINTED IN THE UNITED STATES OF AMERICA

10 9 8 7 6 5 4 3 2 1

THE GUNSMITH

199

DENVER DESPERADOES

PROLOGUE

The ambush was not a surprise to Clint Adams. This was the way his life was. From one moment to the next he never knew when or where the next bullet was coming from. His reaction to the shots was pure reflex. Even as he was throwing himself from the saddle, he grabbed his rifle and took it with him. When he hit the ground he rolled, lead chewing up the ground behind him. Whoever they were, except for one hurried shot to start with, they were pretty good. They were just missing him. Also, from the number of shots there had to be at least two or three, and they all seemed to be decent marksmen.

As he rolled for cover and found it in a gully just off the road he was thinking several things. This had to have been planned, and that meant that someone knew he'd be coming this way. This was not a spur-of-the-moment thing. Either these men had planned this and tracked him—they somehow knew where he was going to be—or someone had hired them.

He settled into his cover. From past experience he knew that they had to come and get him if they wanted him. Also, he knew if he simply stayed there and kept quiet they'd start to wonder if they'd hit him. Eventually, one of them would call out, and then somebody would have to get brave enough to come and take a look.

All of this went through his mind and he knew he was probably in for a vigil of a few hours. He had the patience—after all, it was his life—but he wondered if they did.

Time would tell.

After three hours he was starting to think that either they were more patient than he was, or they had given up and gone off. Why would they have done that? Why wouldn't they check to see if he was dead?

He waited another hour and then decided nobody was that patient. He figured he'd take a chance and stand up. If they had managed to outwait him maybe they deserved another shot at him.

He counted to five and then stood up abruptly. His muscles tensed, either to take a bullet or to fling himself aside again when the shooting started—but it didn't.

He got himself out of the gully and the first thing he did was look for Duke, his big black gelding. The animal knew enough to get away from the shooting, but not to go too far. He found him a couple of hundred yards away, checked him for injury, and then replaced his rifle and mounted up. He thought for a moment of trying to find the place the shooters had fired at him from, but then decided against it. Instead, he decided to count his blessings. He was all right, Duke was uninjured, and the shooters had apparently left. Maybe he'd outwaited them, maybe they'd panicked when they realized they'd missed him. The best thing to do now was to keep going and be extra vigilant. He decided, too, that he'd stay off the main road, in case they were setting up another ambush further on.

Once again he'd managed to avoid a bullet meant for him. There was one out there with his name on it, he knew, but for today he'd managed to come through another ambush.

ONE

Two things had prepared Lyle Calhoun for this time in his life. First, he'd been a bounty hunter for a while, and a very unsuccessful one. He just did not have the knack for it. From bounty hunting he had turned to gambling, and that was something he did have a knack for. Cards just seemed to come to him, but he was smart enough to know that wouldn't last forever. For that reason, when he made his big score, the big one many gamblers wait their lives for, he decided to invest the money in something, but the only other thing he knew was bounty hunting.

And that's when the Ambush League was born. Of course, the name existed in his head only. When he decided to form his little ''club'' or ''league'' he had to call it something, even if it was just in his own head. He thought about the Bounty Hunters Club, but that wasn't quite right. And he liked the word ''league.'' It just sounded more classy.

That was another thing Lyle Calhoun had been

looking for his whole life—some class. He'd had women tell him he didn't have it and never would. They told him he didn't know what it meant to have class, didn't know what it took, but he did. He knew what it took.

Money.

And now he'd found a way to get that.

The Ambush League.

Ambushing a wanted man had been something he'd never been able to do. He couldn't bring himself to put a bullet in a man's back. It just wasn't in him. However, it was in him to pay other men to do it— and that's what his Ambush League was all about.

He picked out the targets, men with prices on their heads, and he sent his men out to ambush them.

"It says dead or alive on the posters," he told the men who worked for him, "and it don't say it's important how they came to be dead."

"So it's okay to shoot them in the back?" one of the men asked.

"It's just fine," Calhoun had said. "In fact, I'd prefer it. It's just easier."

The men he'd hired to work for him looked at each other and nodded.

"Anybody have a problem with that?" he asked.

Now they all exchanged glances and shook their heads. None of them had a problem with that.

"Okay, then," Calhoun had proceeded, "you'll work in threes, so you can watch each other's backs . . ."

He worked out the whole system, taught it to them,

and then sent them out to put it into practice—and it worked. The money came to him and he paid them, and they were all doing better than if they had stayed hunting bounties on their own.

He also warned the men not to go off on their own. If there was somebody they wanted to track down, if it was something personal, they had to come to him with it. If the person fit into the profile he was using, then they could fit him into the program. If not, then the man in question—one of his "agents"—had to forget his personal vendetta, or put it aside for another time. If anyone had a problem with that, he said, they'd better leave right away. No one had left.

At the present time Calhoun had twelve men working for him, in four groups of threes. He stayed in Denver, while they roamed throughout the Southwest. By remaining in a large city rather than a small town, Calhoun was able to keep track of the newly announced rewards and bounties, was able to keep his finger on the pulse of law enforcement through his contacts on the Denver Police Department, and the post office, which had become a wonderful source of wanted posters.

However, Calhoun had broken one of his own rules. Well, he hadn't broken it yet, but he was considering it. He had a personal vendetta against someone who had wronged him, someone he could not hope to overcome face-to-face. The wound had been festering for years, going back to when he was an unsuccessful bounty hunter—and then again, later, as a gambler. All these years he had waited and watched for a chance to take his revenge, and now he thought he had it. But to achieve it, he'd have to break his own rule. If he did that, how could he expect his men to continue to follow him?

Unless there were those among his men he could trust.

So he was at this point. He wanted to approach a couple of his men about this thing but still did not know which ones. For that reason the fulfillment of his vendetta against Clint Adams, the Gunsmith, would have to wait a little longer.

TWO

Clint had a special feeling for three cities in the United States: San Francisco, New York, and Denver. Pressed to pick between the three he'd probably go with San Francisco, but it was a difficult choice.

He rode into Denver from the north three days after the attempted ambush. He'd been extra careful the rest of the way, not trusting the ambushers—the two or three of them—to miss again.

He rode to the hotel where he usually stayed, the Denver House. First he dropped Duke at the livery, where the liveryman remembered the big gelding.

"Always a pleasure to take care of this big boy, Mr. Adams," the man said to him. "Don't you worry about him."

"I won't," Clint said. For the life of him he could not remember the man, but it was obvious that Duke did, because he went with the man as docilely as you please, and that was good enough for Clint.

He entered the huge Denver House lobby and walked to the desk.

"Mr. Adams," the desk clerk said, as if extremely pleased to see him, "how nice to have you with us again."

"It's nice to be here," Clint said. He didn't remember the clerk, either. The clerks in hotels seemed to blend into each other these days. Or maybe he was just getting old, or losing his mind.

"And how long will you be staying with us this time?" the man asked.

"Probably just a day or two," Clint said, signing the register. "I'm really just passing through."

"Oh, too bad." The clerk handed Clint his key. "Enjoy your stay, sir, however long it is. If you need anything just let me know. I'm the assistant manager, John Mason."

"Thanks you, Mr. Mason, I'll let you know," Clint said, accepting the key.

Mason noticed that Clint did not have luggage, just his saddlebags, so he didn't offer Clint a bellboy.

"I'm sure you know the way, sir."

"Yes, thank you, Mr. Mason."

"Just call me John, sir."

"John . . ." Clint said, and made for the stairs.

Clint freshened up and then came down to get something to eat in the hotel dining room, which was one of the best restaurants in Denver. Clint's trips to Denver were too few and far between for him to make many lasting friendships there. The only person he knew would be there from visit to visit was his friend Talbot Roper. Roper was the best private investigator in the United States, bar none—and that included Allan Pinkerton and anyone who worked for him. Other people Clint had met in Denver had usually moved on by the time he came back. But he really came to visit the city, and not anyone who lived in it. He was actually just passing through on his way back to Texas from up north. His ultimate goal was the town of Labyrinth, where he intended to hole up for a while and take a rest from his travels. He knew that would last a few weeks at the most, though, and then he'd be ready to travel again.

He allowed a waiter to seat him and take his order for a steak dinner, a beer, and a newspaper. The beer and newspaper came together, and he sipped one and read the other while he waited for his food. The newspaper was the *Denver Post*, and one article in particular caught his eye. It was about an ambush that had been perpetrated just outside of town. Two or three men had ambushed another, apparently thinking he was a wanted man. After he was dead it turned out to be a case of mistaken identity. The ambushers were being sought, but there were no witnesses. This put Clint in mind of the attempted ambush on him three days ago. Could it have been the same men? And had they also made a mistake with him, not actually known who he was and mistaken him for someone else?

The newspaper said that a detective from the Denver Police Department had been questioned, and that there was not enough information for him to predict an arrest. His name was Detective Michael Rucker. Clint decided that after his meal he'd go and see Detective Rucker and tell the man what had happened to him. It probably wouldn't help much, since Clint had never seen any of the men, but he could tell the detective where it had happened, and maybe they could find out something from the scene.

"Your steak, sir?" the waiter said.

"Hmm? Oh, thank you."

"Anything else, sir?"

"Just get a pot of coffee ready," Clint said. "I'll have it after dinner."

"Yes, sir."

Clint set the newspaper aside and concentrated on his steak dinner. The Denver House served almost as good a steak as the famed Delmonico Steak House, and it deserved all of his attention. He pushed aside any thoughts of ambushers and police detectives and cut into the inch-thick piece of meat.

THREE

Clint entered the police station and approached the front desk.

"Can I help you?" a uniformed policeman asked. He was wearing the three stripes of a sergeant.

"I'd like to see Detective Rucker."

"What's it about?"

"The ambush that was covered in the *Denver Post*," Clint said.

"It was in more newspapers than that," the sergeant commented.

"Well, that's where I saw it."

"And what's your name?"

"Clint Adams."

The sergeant stared at him for a moment then asked, "What was that?"

"Clint Adams."

Again the stare and then the man said, "Wait here."

He left his position behind the desk and returned

several minutes later with another man who was not wearing a uniform, just a dark suit.

"You wanted to see me?"

"Are you Detective Rucker?"

"That's right," Rucker said. "Sergeant Bodeen says you claim to be Clint Adams."

"Why would I claim to be me if I wasn't?" Clint asked.

"Hey," Rucker said, "lots of people like to impersonate other famous people."

"I'm not so famous."

"Yes," Rucker said, "you are. Can you prove who you are?"

"What would you like me to do?" Clint asked. "Shoot somebody?"

"I assume that's a joke."

"I guess this whole idea was a joke," Clint said. "I'm at the Denver House. If you decide to talk to me you can find me there."

With that Clint turned and left the building.

Later Clint chided himself for being so thin-skinned. Why did they have to believe he was who he said he was? The police probably dealt with a lot of crackpots during the course of one day.

He was sitting in the Denver House bar when Detective Rucker entered. The man looked around, located Clint, and walked toward him.

"Can I buy you a drink?" the policeman asked.

Clint looked down at the last remnants of his beer

and said, "I could be persuaded to have another beer."

Rucker went to the bar and came back with two beers.

"Is this an apology?" Clint asked.

"Do you want an apology?"

Clint shook his head.

"It's not necessary. I was being kind of thin-skinned, I guess."

"Well, I was judging too quickly. Should we start over?"

"Sure."

Rucker extended his hand and said, "Mike Rucker."

Clint shook the man's hand and said, "Clint Adams."

"What was it you wanted to see me about, Mr. Adams?"

"Clint."

The detective nodded and said, "Clint."

Briefly, Clint told the man about the attempted ambush three days north of Denver.

"This has happened to you before, hasn't it?" Rucker asked when Clint had finished.

"Of course. It's possible they were just after me for who I was, but I don't like coincidences."

"Well, this would be one," Rucker said. "The ambush in the paper was also north of town."

"Any idea who did it?"

"Oh, yeah," Rucker said, "I have a great idea, I just can't prove it."

"Who?"

"Ever hear of something called the Ambush League?"

"No, should I have?"

"No reason," Rucker said. "You see, no one's heard of it except its members, and me."

"And how did you hear about it?"

"I heard about it from a disgruntled ex-member," Rucker answered.

"Can't he help you prove it?"

"He's dead."

"Oh."

"Yeah, after he talked to me he was killed."

"What about your bosses?"

"They don't believe any such thing exists."

"Well, if it does," Clint said, "somebody thought it up. Who was it?"

"A man named Calhoun."

"Wait a minute," Clint said, sitting up straight in his chair. "Lyle Calhoun?"

"That's him. How'd you know?"

"I know him."

"Well," Rucker said, "this is a coincidence," and Clint made a face.

FOUR

"Tell me what you know about him," Rucker said.

"There's not much to tell, really," Clint said. "He was inept as a bounty hunter. Almost got a friend of mine killed."

"And then what happened?"

"I arranged for him to not get very much work as a bounty hunter."

"That must have put a crimp in his ability to make a living."

"He didn't make a very good living at it to begin with," Clint said. "In fact, as far as I know he wasn't very good at anything, except one thing."

"And what was that?"

"He was lucky at cards," Clint said. "When opportunities as a bounty hunter dried up on him, that's what he turned to."

"And the rest is history, as they say," Rucker said.

"Right," Clint said. "He turned to gambling and

ended up in a big game where a fourth ace found its way into his hand.''

Rucker frowned.

''You sayin' he cheated?''

''I don't think he would have been very good at that, either,'' Clint said. ''No, I'm saying a fourth ace found its way into his hand by luck, and he won a very large sum of money.''

''And started his Ambush League with it.''

''Do you really think so?'' Clint asked. ''I mean, do you absolutely believe your source?''

''I do,'' Rucker said. ''Him getting killed sort of made the difference.''

''And how was he killed?''

''How else?'' Rucker said. ''He was ambushed.''

Rucker stayed through another beer and by the time it was gone Clint still had his doubts.

''I just don't think Calhoun is smart enough to put such a thing together.''

''Maybe being smart was never his problem,'' Rucker offered.

''What do you mean?''

''Well, maybe he was always just physically inept,'' Rucker said. ''Now he's got men who are doing the physical part for him.''

''Could be, I guess,'' Clint admitted reluctantly. ''Where does he live, by the way?''

''Right here in Denver.''

''In the city?''

"That's right."

"What's he supposed to be doing for a living?"

"Can't say I rightly know," Rucker said. "He plays cards, occasionally, but not often enough to be making a living from it. If I'm right about him, then he's collecting on a lot of bounties."

"You can find that kind of thing out. You're the law, after all."

"I tried that," Rucker said. "If he's collecting it's under a different name, or he's got someone doing it for him."

"Can't you find out if one person is collecting a lot of bounties?"

"He's thought of that, too."

"He's probably using different people each time?"

Rucker nodded, and Clint rubbed his jaw thoughtfully.

"Maybe I should stop in and see him."

"What for?"

"Just to say hello."

"You want to shake him up, don't you?"

"Why would I want to do that?"

"Because you're thinking maybe he sent three of his men after you to settle an old score."

"I guess that's possible, too," Clint said.

"How long are you intending to stay in Denver, Clint?" Rucker asked.

Clint looked at the man and then said, "Oh, no, you're not going to drag me into this."

"Who said anything about dragging you into anything?'' the policeman asked defensively. "I just wanted to ask you a favor.''

"What kind of favor?''

"I'd like you to take me back to where you were ambushed.''

"That's three days back in the direction I came,'' Clint complained.

"Oh, I'll bet you were riding easy,'' Rucker said. "On a good horse I'll bet we make it there and back in three days.''

"A good horse?'' Clint asked. "Have you got one?''

"I've got a very good one,'' Rucker said, "and if memory serves, so do you.''

"What do you hope to find?''

"I don't know,'' Rucker said. "I won't know until I get there and take a look. You didn't look the scene over, did you?''

"No,'' Clint said, wishing now that he had.

"Then do this for me and I won't ask you for anything else.''

"Jesus . . .'' Clint said.

FIVE

They agreed to meet early the next morning at the Denver House's livery stable.

"I hope you've got a real good horse," Clint said.

"Don't worry," Rucker said.

"And I hope you can ride."

Rucker smiled at that and said, "I don't think you'll find that a problem."

Rucker left the saloon, and Clint stayed behind to nurse another beer. The place was quiet, because it was a hotel bar, and not a public saloon. Most of the action would be going on in the public places, but Clint wasn't sure he wanted any action.

All of a sudden he had to get up early the next morning.

When Mike Rucker left the hotel there was a man in a doorway across the street watching him. The man didn't follow, he just watched the policeman walk down the block until he was out of sight. When he was, the man crossed the street and entered the hotel.

He'd been inside before, after he'd followed Rucker from the police station. The detective must have had a lot on his mind, because he hadn't looked back once to see if he was being tailed. The man had seen Rucker seat himself at the table with Clint, only at that time he didn't know who Clint was.

The Denver House's night staff was on duty, and the man had a contact there, someone who liked making a little money on the side. It seemed the hotel's night staff was not as squeaky-clean as its day people were.

The man approached the front desk, and the clerk saw him coming and got nervous.

"What are you doing here, Leo?" he demanded in low tones as the man reached the desk. "You want to get me fired?"

"Just pretend I'm asking about room rates," Leo Horton said. "Don't get so nervous."

"What do you want?"

"There's a man in the bar at a back table. I want to know who he is."

"How am I supposed to know who you mean?"

"He's the only man in the place sitting with his back to the wall."

"Oh," the clerk said, a look of recognition crossing his face, "you mean Clint Adams."

"Who?"

"You know, Clint Adams, the Guns—"

"I know who he is," the man said, suddenly thoughtful. "Damn!"

"Do you know him personally?"

"If I knew him would I have to ask you who he is?" Horton replied.

"Oh, that's right."

"When did he get here?"

"Today," the clerk said, "this afternoon."

"How long is he staying?"

"I don't know."

"Why would a policeman be talking to him?" the man asked, but he was actually talking to himself.

"I don't know," the clerk said. Leo Horton ignored him.

"Anything else?" the clerk asked. "I don't want to lose my job."

"Just one more thing," Horton said, leaving a palmed bill on the desk.

The clerk palmed the bill himself smoothly, before anyone could see.

"What?"

"Adams's room number."

"I can't—"

"Did you look at the number on that bill I just gave you?"

Surreptitiously the clerk sneaked a peek and caught his breath. He gave Leo Horton the room number.

SIX

"Come," Lyle Calhoun called when there was a knock on his office door.

Leo Horton entered the room.

"What are you doing here?" Calhoun asked. "I thought you were watching Rucker."

"I was," Horton said, "but this is important."

"What is it?"

Horton didn't answer right away. He eyed the brandy decanter on Calhoun's desk. Since he'd started working for Calhoun he had come to like his boss's expensive taste in liquor.

"Help yourself to a drink, Leo, and tell me what's so important."

Horton poured himself some brandy and sipped it. The first time he'd ever drank it he had downed the glass like a shot of whiskey, but since then Calhoun had instructed him in the proper way to drink it. Calhoun was becoming expert in the proper way of doing a lot of things.

"So? What is it?"

"Clint Adams."

"What about him?"

"He's here. In Denver."

"How do you know?"

"Because Rucker was talking to him tonight."

"What? Where?"

"At the Denver House Hotel."

"Shit."

"I thought you'd be interested."

"Of course I'm interested," Calhoun said, "but what the hell would Adams be doing talking with Rucker?"

"Maybe they were talkin' about you?"

"Me? Why would they be?"

"Well, Rucker's a policeman looking into some killings, and Adams is somebody who knows you."

"But why would my name come up?"

"Maybe Horace said somethin' to Rucker before we got to him, boss."

"Yeah," Calhoun said, rubbing his mouth, which had suddenly gone dry. He poured himself a shot of brandy and downed it like whiskey.

"Hey, I thought you wasn't supposed to do—"

"Shut up, Leo!"

It bothered Calhoun that he didn't know if his mouth had gone dry from anticipation, or fear.

SEVEN

The next morning Clint was waiting outside the livery stable with Duke when Rucker rode up on a big Morgan. The animal was the biggest horse Clint had ever seen, except for Duke and one other.

"He's a gelding," Rucker said, stroking the animal's neck, "five years old. Not as big as your black, but I'll bet he matches his stamina."

"You'll bet?" Clint asked, patting Duke's massive neck. True, the Morgan was almost half Duke's age, but Clint knew that his gelding still had a lot of miles left in him.

"What?"

"You said you'll bet," Clint said. "What will you bet? How much?"

"You mean money?" Rucker asked.

"That's the way a wager usually goes, Mike."

"Well . . ."

"Don't want to back up your words?" Clint asked. "Maybe you're not that confident in your horse."

25

"What did you have in mind?" Rucker said. "I don't have a lot of money."

"Never mind," Clint said, waving the wager away. "I was just kidding."

"No," Rucker said, "I want to bet. I've heard a lot about your horse. I'd like to put mine up against him."

Rucker gave Duke a critical once-over.

"He's big . . . but he's a little old, isn't he?"

"You've got your wager," Clint said, frowning. "Let's discuss the terms on the way."

Rucker's horse's name was Chance. They had cleared the Denver city limits, riding at a good clip but not pushing, before they finally decided on the terms of the wager.

"Okay," Rucker said, "if I win you'll stay in Denver and help me with this whole ambush thing."

"All right," Clint said, "and if I win I get a month's salary."

"Right."

"How much is a month's salary, anyway?"

Rucker told him.

"That's all?" Clint asked. "I think I got gypped."

"Can't back out now," Rucker said.

"I'm not looking to."

"Okay, then," Rucker said. "How do we do this? How do we test them?"

"That's easy," Clint said, kicking Duke gently in the ribs, "just keep up."

Duke shot forward and, before Rucker and his Morgan knew it, they were eating dust.

"Come on, Chance," Rucker said, "let's show this old boy what you've got."

They rode most of the day and Clint had to give Rucker and his horse credit. While distanced, they never really lost touch with Clint and Duke. Finally, Clint reined Duke in and waited for Rucker to catch up. When he did, both he and his mount were out of breath.

"Do you want that month's pay now?" Rucker asked.

"I don't want your month's pay, Rucker," Clint said. "Let's get down off our horses and give them a rest, though."

"Your horse isn't even breathing hard," Rucker complained as he dismounted.

His own horse was blowing so hard they could see his sides heaving.

"Where does he get the stamina?"

Clint patted Duke's neck and said, "I guess it comes with old age."

"Okay," Rucker said, "I'm sorry I said anything about him being old."

Rucker took his canteen from his saddle and drank some water. Then he poured some into his hat and let his horse drink.

"How far are we from where you were ambushed?" he asked.

"Not that far, really," Clint said, "but I think we'll

have to camp soon and then cover the rest of the ground tomorrow. We should be there by noon.''

"See?" Rucker said. "I told you a couple of good horses could make it in a day and a half.''

"Chance is a good horse, all right,'' Clint said. "Duke would have left most horses completely behind and out of sight. I don't think we should push either one of them that hard anymore, though.''

"That suits me.''

"I'll say one thing, though,'' Clint said. "You can ride.''

"Been riding all my life,'' Rucker said. "Still, being a city detective has kept me out of the saddle for a while. I think by the time we get back to Denver my butt will be plenty sore.''

"Come on,'' Clint said. "We'll ride a little further and then camp for the night. I've got some beef jerky and coffee in my saddlebags.''

"Good,'' Rucker said. "I'm glad one of us thought to bring it.''

EIGHT

"This is it."

It was just after noon the next day when Clint reined Duke in.

"Are you sure?"

"I took cover in that gully," Clint said, pointing. "I was there for hours."

"And they never fired again?"

"No."

"Never came down?"

"No."

"Did they call out to you?"

"Not a word."

Rucker stood in his stirrups and looked around.

"Where do you think they were?"

Clint pointed again.

"I'd say they were up there," he said, indicating a nearby hill. "It's the only ground high enough for any decent ambush."

"I guess we'd better take a look then."

• • •

When they reached the top of the hill it was obvious from the tracks on the ground that Clint had chosen the right place.

"Lucky it hasn't rained in a while," Rucker said.

"Got some distinct boot tracks here, Detective."

"Why don't you just call me Michael," Rucker suggested.

"All right," Clint said. "I guess we know each other well enough to be on a first-name basis by now."

"Clint," Rucker said, "I'm no master tracker. Why don't you tell me what you see."

Clint looked at the ground.

"I see three men, all good size, or else they've all got big feet, and they're all about thirty-five."

"What?" Rucker asked. "How do you know how old they are?"

"I don't," Clint said. "I just made that up."

Rucker looked relieved.

"Well, I could tell there were three of them, but that's about all. How many of them fired at you?"

"I think they each fired once," Clint said.

"And they all missed?"

"That's obvious."

"No, what I mean is, the word I got is that all of the men Calhoun is using are good. How could all three men have missed?"

"Let me think," Clint said, playing the scene over in his head. "I think one of the shots came a split second ahead of the other two."

"So one of them jumped the gun, so to speak," Rucker said, "probably in haste."

"No, if they were Calhoun's men and as good as you say that wouldn't have happened."

"So what are you saying?"

"That one of them fired first on purpose."

"As a warning?"

Clint nodded.

"That means we've got somebody in the other camp," Rucker said. "If we could find out who he is he'd help us."

"Maybe," Clint said.

"Why maybe?"

"Just because he didn't want to back-shoot me doesn't mean he'd help you."

Clint hated back-shooters, and had hated them since his friend Jim Hickok—aka Wild Bill—had been killed by one. Ambushers—or bushwhackers—were barely a step up from back-shooters, in his estimation. It was a sign that he was mellowing that he hadn't tried to track these particular ambushers down, but he'd had no idea at the time whether they were still in the area or not. Three to one odds, even for him, were not good.

Now, however, he could see the trail the men had left, leading down the hill.

"Can you track them?" Rucker asked, also noticing the trail.

"I don't see why not," Clint said.

"Now?" Rucker asked.

Clint nodded and said, "Now."

• • •

As it turned out tracking them wasn't a bad idea because the tracks led back toward Denver. They followed them until dusk—losing them a couple of times
but then finding them again—and then camped and
once again made a meal of jerky and coffee.

"What would you do to them if you found them?"
Rucker asked.

"There was a time I would have killed them on the
spot," Clint said.

"Well," Rucker said, "that would put me in a bad
position."

"Now I'd probably just turn them over to you,
alive."

"That would be a big help."

"There's another possibility, you know," Clint
said.

"What's that?"

"That these men don't work for Calhoun. After all,
there's no profit for Calhoun in sending three of his
men to kill me."

"No monetary profit, you mean," Rucker said.
"There's still revenge."

"After all this time?" Clint asked. "I doubt that
Calhoun would hold a grudge this long."

"You made it sound as if you humiliated him."

"Humiliated?" Clint said, thinking back. "That's
a pretty harsh word, I think."

"Not to the men I know," Rucker said. "Most men
don't take that kind of thing lightly."

Clint poured himself another cup of coffee, thoughtfully.

"If Calhoun did send those men after me," Clint said, "I can't just ride away and forget about it."

"Does that mean you'll stay in Denver awhile?" Rucker asked hopefully.

Clint swirled the coffee in his cup for a few moments before answering.

"Long enough to pay a visit to Calhoun," he finally answered. "You do know where he lives, don't you?"

"Oh, yeah," Rucker said. "Where he lives, what men's club he belongs to."

"Good."

"But why do you want to visit him?" Rucker asked. "To do what?"

"Oh, to talk," Clint said, smiling at the detective, "just to talk."

Rucker was glad the smile wasn't actually meant for him.

NINE

The trail eventually led to a small wooden shack about twenty miles north of Denver. They dismounted, walked their horses far enough away so as not to give them away, then approached the shack again and studied it.

"Think they're in there?" Rucker asked.

"Probably not," Clint said. "No horses, unless they're behind the shack. Also, no smoke from the chimney. Still, there could be someone inside. Let's approach it real careful."

"Right."

"I'll go around back," Clint said, "and since you're the lawman here, you can take the front."

"Sounds fair. Say, aren't you friends with Talbot Roper?"

Clint looked at the detective.

"What's that got to do with anything?"

Rucker shrugged and said, "It's just a question that occurred to me."

"Well, ask your questions later."

"Right. Let's move."

Clint looked at the gun Rucker had produced from inside his jacket. It was a Colt that he had cut down so that it would fit in his jacket.

"Can you hit anything with that?" Clint asked.

"Only what I aim at."

"Aim?"

Rucker nodded.

"We'll have to talk later." Clint was of the school that said you didn't "aim" a gun you "pointed" it, like your finger.

They separated and Clint moved around behind the shack. There were no horses. That was good. As he got closer he saw the tracks that horses had made on the ground, and noticed that they did not lead to or from Denver.

When he reached the back of the shack he stole a peek in a window and saw Rucker standing in the doorway. The shack was empty. Clint walked around to the front and entered.

"Nobody home," Rucker said.

"I can see that. There's a jumble of tracks outside, but they don't lead to Denver."

"We can follow them."

Clint shook his head.

"Not without provisions, and a posse. There were a lot of horses here, at least eight or nine. I'm not tracking that many men without some help."

"You're right, of course," Rucker said. "And nine

men sounds right. That would make it three groups of three, all working for Calhoun.''

"I hope you don't have Calhoun on the brain.''

"What does that mean?''

"Just that you've got to keep an open mind, Mike,'' Clint said. "Everything can't be Calhoun's doing.''

"I've got an open mind,'' Rucker said, putting his gun away, "but the name Calhoun keeps jumping into it. Let's take a look around and see what we can find.''

They did a quick search of the place, found some empty fruit and coffee cans, but not much else.

"This place is not telling us anything,'' Rucker complained.

"Come back with a posse,'' Clint suggested, "and somebody who can track.''

"Not you?''

Clint shook his head.

"I'm staying in Denver to have a talk with Calhoun, remember?''

"What are you gonna ask him?''

"I'm going to ask him if he sent three men to kill me,'' Clint said, "and suggest that he think twice before doing it again. I'm going to tell him that if anyone so much as shoots a dirty look my way in the next year I'll hold him personally responsible.''

"That's great,'' Rucker said. "After that, he'll have to kill you.''

TEN

When they got back to Denver they split up at the Denver House. It was late afternoon, almost time for dinner, so Clint said, "I'll come into the station tomorrow and get Calhoun's address from you—that is, unless you have it memorized."

"I don't." It was a lie and Clint knew it, but he let Rucker have it. The man wanted to think on it first before he gave the address to him. Maybe he thought Clint meant to kill Calhoun on sight.

"That's a nice horse," Clint said to Rucker as the man started to ride away.

"Thanks."

"He'll be an even nicer one when he gets a bit older." Clint tossed this last remark at the man's retreating back, and Rucker did not respond to it.

Clint took Duke into the hotel livery and tended to him himself.

•   •   •

Mike Rucker took his horse to the livery where he
boarded him and then went to his office. Actually, he
didn't have an office of his own, he shared it with
several other men. His boss had an office, though, and
he found a message on his desk that Inspector Jameson wanted to see him.

He knocked on Jameson's door and asked, ''You
wanted to see me, boss?''

Jameson looked up from his desk and beckoned the
younger man to enter. Jameson had been a lawman in
Denver most of his life. First as a deputy, then a sher-
iff, and when the Metropolitan force was formed he
was one of its first officers. He had spent thirty years
in law enforcement, and every one of them was etched
on his face.

''Come in and sit down, Rucker.''

''Yes, sir.''

Jameson pushed away the reports he'd been reading
and lit a cigar. There were still ashes on the front of
his shirt from his last cigar. He had a decent-sized
belly on him, swelling the front of his white shirt, and
it usually kept his ashes from falling to the floor—
that is, until he stood up.

''What's happening with the ambush murder?''

''I still like Calhoun for it.''

Jameson shook his head.

''You've got no proof.''

''I'm working on it.''

''Doing what?''

''I'm . . . I've questioned a man who recently came
to town and knows Calhoun.''

"Oh? Who's that?"

"Clint Adams."

Jameson sat forward, and the old and new ash fell to the floor.

"The Gunsmith?"

"That's right."

"What's he got to do with Calhoun?"

"They have a history."

"What kind of history?"

"An adversarial one."

"In English, Detective."

"Not a friendly one."

"Ah. And what do you propose to do with this information?"

"I don't know yet, sir," Rucker said.

"Where is Adams staying?"

"The Denver House."

"Until when?"

"He doesn't know," Rucker said. "He's passing through, may stay a day or two."

"I see. Is he going to see Calhoun while he's here?" the inspector asked.

"That I don't know, sir," Rucker said. It was his day for telling lies.

"Well, find out," Jameson said. "I don't want the Gunsmith killing him before we can prove something against him."

"Yes, sir."

"That's all, then," Jameson said, sitting back again. "Keep working on it."

"Yes, sir."

Rucker got up and left Jameson's office. The inspector sat back and regarded the glowing tip of his cigar. In fact, he blew on it so it would continue to glow while he ran through his thoughts.

The Gunsmith was in Denver. He wondered if Calhoun knew that. He wondered what it would be worth to the man. Jameson hadn't lasted thirty years as a lawman without always making the best of his position. He certainly couldn't have survived all those years just on the money he made from his job. No, there always had to be "sidelines" to the work. Now he was coming to the end of his career, he knew. Nearly sixty, he wasn't going to be doing this for much longer. He was going to be moved out to make room for the younger men, like Rucker. Rucker was a honest policeman and would probably make inspector before he was forty. Jameson had to make the most of the position while he still had it. He'd started doing that a couple of years ago, by keeping an eye on who was coming into power in Denver. He'd spotted Calhoun early and had latched on to him.

He piled the reports on his desk and pushed them into a corner, then stood up and left the building, taking his cigar with him.

ELEVEN

Calhoun stared across his desk at Inspector Ben Jameson. The policeman had one of his foul-smelling cigars going, and Calhoun knew he was going to have to clean ashes from the floor when the man left—and open a window.

"What is it, Inspector?" Calhoun asked. "What brings you right to my door in broad daylight? I thought you were more subtle than that."

Jameson picked a piece of tobacco from his tongue and examined it, then flicked it away. Calhoun cringed.

"I can't afford to be subtle, Calhoun," Jameson said. "Retirement is comin' up real quick."

"Ah," Calhoun said, nodding his head, "time for you to make a deposit into your retirement fund?"

"Exactly."

"And you have a piece of information you think I might pay for?"

"Right again."

"And would this information have anything to do with Clint Adams being in town?"

"Huh?" Calhoun enjoyed the way Jameson's face dropped.

"And the fact that he's been in the company of your Detective Rucker?"

Jameson sat back, his look now an unhappy one.

"I'm sorry, Inspector, that you can't turn that information into money," Calhoun said.

"Yeah," Jameson said, "I'll bet you are."

"But I'll tell you what I will pay you for."

"Adams's hotel?" Jameson asked hopefully.

Calhoun smiled and said, "The Denver House."

"What are you gonna pay for, then, if you know everything already?"

"I understand your Detective Rucker is after me."

"He's not my detective, but you're right about that. He likes you for that ambush murder."

"But he can't prove it."

"No," Jameson said, "his only witness turned up dead."

"Too bad."

"You still haven't told me what you'll pay me for."

"Just keep Rucker busy with other things," Calhoun said. "Don't give him enough time to work on me."

"That's all?"

"That's it."

"And how much is that worth to you?"

Calhoun named a figure.

"That much?"

"That much."

Suddenly, Jameson's impending retirement did not seem so grim, after all.

TWELVE

The next morning Clint had breakfast in the Denver House dining room and then went to the police station where he'd met Mike Rucker. The same policeman was working the desk when he asked for the detective.

"He's not here."

"When will he be in?"

The man shrugged.

"The boss gave him some jobs to do today," he said. "Don't know when he'll be back."

"Who's his boss?"

"Inspector Jameson."

"Then can I see him?"

"He ain't in yet."

"Then when did he give Rucker these jobs?"

"Last night," the policeman said, "before they both went home. Mister, I got my own work to do."

"Okay, all right," Clint said, "thanks."

He turned to leave.

"Hey, wait," the policeman said. "Is your name Clint Adams?"

"That's right."

"Well, Rucker left this for you."

He held out an envelope and Clint took it.

"Thanks."

Clint waited until he got outside to read the note in the envelope. It said "Lyle Calhoun" and had an address. Clint smiled, put the note back in the envelope, and then put it in his pocket. He grabbed one of the cabs sitting in front of the police station and gave the driver the address.

"Fella outside wants to see you, boss," Leo said to Calhoun.

"Who is it?"

"Says he's an old friend."

Calhoun gave Leo a hard stare.

"It's Adams," Leo finally said.

"Show him in, Leo."

Clint entered the room and Calhoun's heart suddenly started beating faster. He had a gun in his desk drawer and he almost went for it. He knew that would be foolish, though. That would give Adams a reason to kill him. As long as he didn't have a gun, he knew Clint Adams wouldn't shoot him in cold blood. He wasn't that kind of man.

"Clint," he said, "how nice to see you."

"Is it, Lyle?" Clint asked.

"Well, sure, why wouldn't it be?"

Clint looked around at the expensive furnishings in the room.

"I just thought you might still be holding a grudge."

"A grudge? Oh, I see what you mean. No, no, I forgot about that stuff a long time ago."

"Did you?"

"Sure," Calhoun said. "How about a drink?"

"No, thanks."

Calhoun looked past Clint to the door, where Leo was still standing, leaning against the wall.

"That's all, Leo. You can go."

Leo stood straight and left the room, closing the door behind him. Calhoun sat behind his desk. Clint remained standing.

"What brings you here, Clint?"

"You seem to have done very nicely for yourself, Lyle," Clint said, instead of answering the question.

"I do all right."

"Got yourself a nice little stake, I heard."

Calhoun smiled and spread his hands.

"The cards were running my way," he said. "What can I say?"

"You don't seem very surprised to see me. Why is that?" Clint asked.

"I have a lot of eyes and ears in this city, Clint," Calhoun said. "I knew you were here as soon as you checked into your hotel."

Clint knew it hadn't been that soon, but figured it wasn't much longer than that.

"You've become a big man, huh?"

"Big enough."

"Big enough to have other men do your killing for you?" Clint asked.

"Killing?" Calhoun asked. "What are you talking about?"

"Three men tried to kill me the other day, Lyle," Clint said, "from ambush. That ring a bell with you?"

"Why should it?"

"Seems to me that was the way you worked when you were hunting bounties."

"I don't hunt bounties anymore, Clint."

"No, that's right," Clint said, "you get other people to do it for you, don't you? From ambush."

"I don't know where you get your information, Clint—"

"How about from the police?"

"Ah," Calhoun said, "now I understand. You've been talking to a police detective named Rucker."

"Have I?"

"Sure," Calhoun said, "he's the only one who would be telling you these things. He's got it in for me, for some reason."

"Maybe it's because he doesn't like lawbreakers."

"What would that have to do with me?" Calhoun said. "I haven't broken any laws lately."

"Okay, Lyle," Clint said, "let me get to the reason I'm here."

"I wish you would," Calhoun said. "I have a pretty busy day ahead of me."

"Three men tried to kill me," Clint said. "I have reason to believe they work for you."

"Who are they?"

"I don't know."

"Then how can you figure they work for me?" Calhoun asked. "Really, Clint, you're not being very fair here."

"I'm not looking to be fair, Lyle," Clint said. "I have to look over my shoulder enough because of my reputation. I don't need to be looking specifically for your men."

"Clint—"

"I'm just going to tell you this once, Lyle," Clint said, not letting the man talk. "If I get shot at again, I'm coming after you."

"Now that's really not fair, Clint," Calhoun said. "I'll bet there's somebody every day who wants to take a shot at you."

"Well, you'd better hope they don't," Clint said, "especially not while I'm here in Denver."

"How long do you intend to stay?" Calhoun asked. "Maybe we can have dinner—"

"I said what I came to say, Calhoun," Clint said. "Just think about it."

With that Clint turned and walked toward the door. Calhoun was sorely tempted to pull the gun from his drawer and shoot Clint in the back, but he was afraid to, pure and simple. Sometimes men like Clint Adams seemed to have eyes in the back of their heads.

After Clint left Leo returned to the room.

"What did he want?"

"He wanted to tell me that three men tried to ambush him,'' Calhoun said. ''Do you know anything about that, Leo?''

''Not me, boss.''

''Tell the others I want to see them.''

''Why would any of us try to ambush him? He ain't got a price on his head.''

''That's what I want to find out, Leo. Get the others here!'' Calhoun shouted.

''Okay, boss, okay,'' Leo said. ''I'll get them here. Seems to me, though, if somebody did kill Adams they'd be doing you a big favor.''

''If they shot at him and hit him, yes,'' Calhoun said. ''But whoever did it shot and missed, and if they try it again and miss he's going to come after me.''

''Is that what he said?''

''That's what he said.''

''Geez, boss—''

''Just go and do what I told you to do!''

''I'm going, boss, I'm going,'' Leo said, and hurried out the door.

''Damn it!'' Calhoun swore. He would have taken care of Adams in his own time, but now somebody had pushed the play, and he wanted to find out who the hell it was.

THIRTEEN

When Clint returned to the Denver House he was surprised to find Detective Mike Rucker waiting for him in the lobby. As Clint approached, the policeman stood up from the plush lobby sofa he was sitting on.

"I'm surprised to find you here," Clint said.

"Why's that?"

"I went by the station this morning. They told me your boss gave you some jobs to do."

"Shit jobs," Rucker said. "Inspector Jameson is trying to keep me from working on Lyle Calhoun."

"Why would he do that?" Clint asked, afraid he already knew the answer.

"Money."

"You mean he's taking money from Calhoun?"

"Calhoun is just one in a long line of men he's taken money from, Clint. In fact, half the Denver police force is taking money from somebody—criminal, politician, madam. Everybody's got their hand in somebody's pocket."

"Why don't we get a drink?" Clint suggested, and they went into the hotel bar.

They didn't speak again until they were seated at a back table with a beer in front of each of them. It was early and there was only one other customer present. He was also at a table, hunched over a beer, and may have been asleep. He also could have been dead, but Clint decided not to check.

"So half your police force is crooked?"

Rucker nodded.

"You know which half?"

Now the man shook his head.

"So you don't know who to trust."

"I've got other resources," Rucker said. "Just haven't had a reason to use them yet. How did your meeting go with Calhoun?"

Clint outlined it briefly while drinking half his beer.

"So he didn't deny sending three men after you," Rucker said when Clint was done.

"Didn't admit it, either."

"What do you think?"

Clint mulled it over a moment.

"I think three of his men tried to ambush me," Clint said, "but I don't think he knew anything about it."

"What?"

"I think when I told him what happened he was surprised."

"So why would they do that?"

"Trying to please their boss," Clint said.

"And if he didn't tell them to do it?"

"Then somebody's going to get raked over the coals today."

"That means that if I was outside his home I'd be able to see them, and identify them later."

"Only you've got other things to do," Clint said, "courtesy of your crooked boss."

"You know those other resources I told you about?"

Clint nodded.

"Maybe it's time I tapped them. They could take care of the shit jobs for me while I concentrate on Calhoun."

"What are these other resources?"

"Just some street people."

"And they'd work with a policeman?"

"A policeman who doesn't treat them like lepers."

"Sounds interesting. Maybe I'll stick around awhile. You could use me as one of your resources."

"I'd appreciate that," Rucker said. "What made you change your mind?"

"Just thought I'd stay over a few days more, that's all," Clint said. "Maybe see some friends."

"That was something else I wanted to talk to you about."

"What's that?"

"Well, you have a friend who might be able to help us some."

"Talbot Roper," Clint said without hesitation.

"That's the one," Rucker said. "Do you think he'd help? If you asked him?"

"He probably would," Clint said. "The question is, though, will I ask him?"

"Why wouldn't you? I thought you were friends."

"I don't have so many friends that I can just ask them to drop everything and help me. Friends like that you start to avoid."

"Guess I just don't know that much about having friends."

"Tell you what," Clint said. "I'll have a talk with Roper and see what he says. I want to stop in and see him, anyway."

"Today?"

"Yes, today."

"That's great," Rucker said, pushing away his empty mug and standing up. "I'll go and mobilize those other resources I told you about. If they get busy I can probably be in front of Calhoun's place in a couple of hours."

"Why don't we meet back here in two hours, then," Clint suggested. "I should know something by then, too."

"Okay, then," Rucker said, "two hours, right here."

Clint remained seated while the policeman left the bar, and the hotel. Now all he had to do was find out if Roper was in town.

FOURTEEN

Clint expected to see a new face in Talbot Roper's office, and he wasn't disappointed. Roper went through young, pretty secretaries by the dozens, and the funny thing about it was they were always as smart as they were pretty. This one was blond, in her twenties, short and bosomy, with blue eyes that fastened themselves to him as soon as he walked in and never wavered.

"Can I help you?"

"What's your name?"

"Amy," she said. "What's yours?"

"Clint."

She pointed her pencil at him and said, "Adams."

"Right."

"Mr. Roper warned me about you."

"He did? What did he say?"

"That you'd walk through that door and the first thing you'd do was tell me lies about him."

"What was the second thing he told you I'd say?"

"Probably lies about you," she said. "Do you want to see him?"

"Is he here?"

"That depends," she said, "on whether or not he wants to see you."

"Why don't we ask him?"

"I think that's always the best way to find out," she said, standing up, "don't you? I'll just be a minute."

"I'll wait right here."

She went into Roper's office and closed the door behind her, only to reappear seconds later.

"Well," she said, "apparently I was supposed to already know that he'd see you. You can go in."

Clint smiled, said, "Excuse me," and slid past her. Her firm breasts brushed against him as he did, but she didn't seem to mind—or notice, for that matter.

"Clint, you son of a gun, why didn't you tell that girl to let you in?"

Clint crossed the room and shook his friend's hand across his desk.

"Did you yell at her?"

"Maybe a little."

"How long have you had this one?"

"Who knows?" Roper asked. "Months? Weeks? They all blend together. Have a seat."

Roper was tall, broad-shouldered, had dark hair peppered through with more gray than last time Clint had seen him. There also seemed to be more lines on his ruggedly handsome face, but they didn't hurt him any.

"You know a man named Calhoun?"

Roper nodded and said, "Lyle Calhoun. What about him?"

"Do you know what he does for a living?"

"Sure I do," Roper said, "but I can't prove it, and neither can the police."

"Are we talking about the same thing?"

"As I understand it," Roper said, "he likes to call it his 'Ambush League.' Cute name, huh?"

"Not if you're on the receiving end of the ambush," Clint said.

"And you were?"

"Nearly."

Clint told Roper the story in a few short sentences.

"What do you want me to do?"

"Be available, I guess," Clint said. "I've agreed to work with a young detective named Rucker."

"Michael Rucker," Roper said. "I've heard good things about him."

"Like?"

"Well, for one, he's honest. That's a rarity these days."

"When did that happen?" Clint asked. "I mean, when did the police department become so corrupt?"

"You've never lived here, Clint," Roper said. "It's always been corrupt to a certain degree, but it's getting progressively worse."

"Rucker reports to a man named Jameson."

"I know Jameson," Roper said. "He's been a lawman around here since before there was a police department."

"A crooked lawman?"

Roper shrugged.

"Maybe he took a dime here and there to turn his head," Roper said. "Does that make him crooked?"

"It does in my book."

"Well, not compared to what's going on now. What are you and young Mr. Rucker preparing to do?"

"Identify some of the members of this league, if we can."

"My guess is Rucker would have to see them himself so he could identify them."

"Right," Clint said. "We're taking steps to do that now. He did ask, though, if you'd be willing to help. Will you be in town?"

Roper spread his hands.

"I don't anticipate going anywhere for a few weeks, when I have to be in Washington. So I guess I'm all yours. Just call when you need me."

"Rucker apparently has some street resources."

"Smart man," Roper said. "The street people know what's going on."

"If we need you, he'll probably send one of them."

"No problem," Roper said. "There's a good chance I'll know whoever he sends."

"I appreciate this, Tal."

Both men stood and shook hands again.

"What are friends for?"

"Not to ask constant favors, that's for sure," Clint said.

"Anytime, Clint," Roper said. "I know you'd do the same for me."

And in point of fact, Clint knew that he would.

Roper walked Clint out.

"Before you leave we'll get a steak," he said, with his hand on Clint's shoulder.

"Under one condition," Clint said.

"What's that?"

"You give this young lady a raise."

Amy looked up at them in surprise.

"What for?" Roper asked.

"Because she has to put up with you."

"What do you think, Amy?" Roper asked. "Do you deserve a raise?"

"Probably not, sir," she said. "I've only been here a short while."

"See what an honest girl she is?" Roper asked.

"Valuable, that kind of honesty," Clint said.

"You're right," Roper said, then looked at Amy. "All right, my girl, you have a raise, compliments of my friend here, Mr. Adams."

"How much?" she asked, looking at Clint.

"Well," Clint said, "I've done enough damage here. I think I'll leave that to you and your boss."

FIFTEEN

Lyle Calhoun looked up from his desk as Leo entered the room. He hadn't been doing anything, just staring at the desktop.

"What?" he demanded.

"Hedge is here, with Deke and Brannon."

"Send them in."

Calhoun had twelve men working for him, riding in threes. Hedge, Deke, and Brannon were not his top three, they weren't even second or third. This was his last team, one with which he had been playing with for the past few months. Hedge was the only one who had been there from the start. Calhoun kept moving men out and bringing others in, hoping to put together a team he could depend on. So far that hadn't happened, and he was thinking maybe it was time to replace Hedge.

Jim Hedge had been a bounty hunter for years, and while not the best in the business he had certainly been better at it than Calhoun. As Hedge entered Cal-

59

houn was surprised to see that the man's hair had gone completely gray. Had this happened just since he'd last seen him, or had Hedge gone gray without Calhoun noticing? How old was he anyway? Fifty? More?

Behind Hedge came the other two, Deke Preston and Barney Brannon. They were both younger than Hedge by a lot, in their early thirties, and they were taller and more slender than he was.

"You wanted to see us?" Hedge asked.

"Got a job for us, boss?" Brannon asked.

"I've got a question for you three and I need an honest answer."

"Go ahead," Hedge said, "ask."

"Any of you three fired a shot at a man named Clint Adams?"

"Adams?" Hedge repeated.

"The Gunsmith," Brannon said helpfully.

"I know who Adams is, Brannon," Hedge growled. "Why do you ask? Has he been shot?"

"I didn't know there was a price on his head," Deke Preston said.

"There isn't, and he hasn't been shot, he's been shot at."

"What's that to us?" Hedge asked.

"That's what I'm asking," Calhoun said. "He thinks I had something to do with it. Now, answer the question."

"Hell," Brannon said, "I wouldn't be crazy enough to shoot at the Gunsmith even if he did have a price on his head."

"Hedge?" Calhoun said.

"I didn't do it, boss."

Calhoun looked at Preston.

"Hell, not me, boss," Preston said. "I ain't lookin' to get killed."

"All right," Calhoun said. "You can leave."

"That's it?" Hedge asked. "That's all you called us here for?"

"That's it."

Preston and Brannon turned and left, but Hedge lingered.

"Has the Gunsmith got a price on his head now?"

"No."

"Then why would he think you had something to do with it?"

"We had a beef a while back," Calhoun said.

"Oh, that's right," Hedge said. "You mentioned that when you first hired me."

"Did I?" Calhoun wondered why he had done that, and if he'd mentioned it to anyone else.

"Yeah, you did."

"I don't remember that. You can go, Hedge."

"Sure."

"Hey, Hedge?"

The man stopped at the door and turned around.

"Yeah?"

"How old are you?"

"What's that got to do with anything?"

"I'm just curious."

"I'm fifty-two."

"Okay," Calhoun said, and the man left, shaking his head.

When had Hedge even turned fifty? Calhoun himself was forty-four, and couldn't quite remember what it had been like when he turned forty.

When Calhoun got in a mood like this—wondering about life, thinking that he was getting old—it was time for a woman.

"Leo?" he bellowed.

Leo appeared at the door.

"I'm going out."

"Where, boss?"

"Lillian's."

"Want some company?" Leo almost leered. Lillian's was the most expensive whorehouse in Denver.

"No," Calhoun said, standing up. "I'll be back in a little while. If any of the others show up have them wait."

"Any idea how long you'll be?"

"As long as it takes."

As Calhoun left the office, Leo was thinking, no telling how long that'd be.

SIXTEEN

Clint and Rucker had met at the Denver House and gotten to Calhoun's house in time to see three men leave.

"Recognize any of them?" Clint asked.

"Just one," Rucker said, "the older one. Looks like a man named Hedge."

"Jim Hedge?"

"That's right," Rucker said. "How do you know him?"

"Well, if it's the Jim Hedge I'm thinking of he's been a bounty hunter for a long time. Must be nearly fifty by now."

"Sounds about right."

"What's he doing working for Calhoun? Calhoun was never anywhere near the bounty hunter Hedge was—and Hedge wasn't that good. He was crude and brutal."

"Like you said," Rucker replied, "he's nearly

fifty, if not fifty, already. Guess he's lookin' to take it a bit easier.''

"And ambushing people is easier than what he used to do," Clint finished.

"I don't know the other two," Rucker said, "but I'd know them again if I saw them, which is the whole point of bein' here."

"Here" was a doorway across the street from Calhoun's building.

"I guess he's calling his men in to talk to them," Rucker said, "and these were the first."

"Can't be his first team," Clint said. "Not with Hedge in it."

"Would Hedge want to kill you for any reason?" Rucker asked.

"Nothing personal," Clint said.

"Well, I guess we'd better settle in and wait for the others to show."

Just as he said that, however, the door opened across the street and Calhoun stepped out.

"He's leaving?" Rucker said.

They watched as Calhoun walked to the street and looked for a cab. He shrugged when he didn't see one coming, turned and started walking away from them.

"Jesus," Rucker said, "I'd better follow him. He might be going to meet the others."

"I'll follow him," Clint said quickly. "It makes more sense that the others would be coming here. Maybe he's not going to be gone that long."

"Okay," Rucker said, "I won't argue because if I do he'll get away. Go ahead."

"See you soon."

"Don't get spotted!"

"I won't."

Clint followed Calhoun on a twenty-minute walk, and then Calhoun mounted the steps of a three-story stone building and entered, pulling the bell.

Clint crossed the street and found a deep doorway he could melt into. He didn't know what this building was, but he couldn't afford to go inside. His only play was to stay here and wait.

Inside Calhoun gave his coat to a lovely, dark-haired young woman in a flimsy nightgown. She was very slender, with small breasts and slim hips, not his type at all, except for the fact that she could have been sixteen. She wasn't, he knew, because Lillian did not have underage girls in her place, but Nina *could* have passed.

"Nice to see you again, Mr. Calhoun."

"Thank you, Nina."

"Are you going to let me go upstairs with you today?" Nina teased. Calhoun was a very good paying customer, and Lillian had given instructions to all the girls to fuss over him and flirt with him.

"I'm afraid not today, Nina."

"One day," she said, "one day, Mr. Calhoun, you'll let me show you what you're missing."

"One day," he said, patting her cheek. "Where's Lillian?"

"With the girls in the parlor, Mr. Calhoun."

"Thank you, Nina."

As Calhoun left the foyer for the parlor, Nina heaved a sigh of relief that she had once again gotten away with her offer. One of these days, though, he was going to take her up on it, and she wasn't looking forward to that day.

As Clint watched he noticed that only men went in and came out of the building. The men who went in had an anxious, anticipatory look on their faces, and the men leaving looked extremely happy and satisfied with themselves. For this reason he was fairly certain that it was a cathouse. Calhoun must have gotten himself an afternoon urge to leave his home even though his men were coming to see him.

Clint thought it would be interesting to see how long Calhoun stayed inside.

SEVENTEEN

Calhoun entered the parlor and was immediately besieged by women in all stages of undress. Lillian, a fortyish, matronly looking woman who owned and operated the place, had to save him, sending the girls scurrying back to their sofas and chairs. Calhoun knew they fussed over him because he was a good paying customer, and he didn't care. Women like this would not have given him another look, otherwise.

"Mr. Calhoun," Lillian said, taking his arm, "so nice of you to visit us again."

Her hands were plump and adorned with rings, the stones of which winked as she gestured.

"Lillian," Calhoun said, "I thought we agreed you'd call me Lyle."

"Lyle it is, then," Lillian said. "There are my girls, Lyle. Who is your pleasure?"

He looked around. There were blondes, redheads, brunettes; girls with pale skin, olive skin, black skin;

short girls, tall girls, skinny girls, plump girls; and girls—and women—of all ages.

"Where is Tanya?" he said.

"I'm sorry," Lillian said, "but Tanya went upstairs with a customer just a few moments before you arrived."

He made a face but not a fuss. The last thing he wanted was to be banned from Lillian's, and he knew men who had suffered that fate simply for stating their disappointment. Lillian wanted no unsatisfied customers in her place.

Tanya was Calhoun's favorite because she was as small and young-looking as Nina, the dark-haired girl at the door, but she also had plump breasts and sweet, round buttocks.

He looked around and found the next best thing to Tanya. She was a redhead named Rusty, and she had the sweet, angelic face of a fourteen-year-old, but the body of a woman.

"Rusty."

"Good choice," Lillian said. "Rusty, honey?" she called out.

Rusty got up from the sofa and walked slowly over to Lillian and Calhoun.

"Please, enjoy your stay, Lyle," Lillian said, surrendering Calhoun's arm to Rusty.

"How are you today, Mr. Calhoun?" Rusty asked, leading him from the parlor.

"Not doing all that well, Rusty," Calhoun said, "but I expect things to get better in the next few minutes."

"I expect they will, Mr. Calhoun," Rusty said with a laugh, "I expect they will."

A few minutes later Calhoun was lying on his back in Rusty's bed and she was down between his legs, studiously working on him with her mouth and tongue. The girls exchanged information about Lillian's customers for times just like this, when Tanya wasn't available for Calhoun. Rusty knew what Calhoun liked. She sucked him and caressed him and called him "Daddy" because Calhoun liked to think he was in bed with a little girl. The more she called him "Daddy" the closer he got to orgasm, and finally, while she was sucking him, he ejaculated. She released him from her mouth so that he shot all over her body, something else he liked.

"Did you like that?" he asked her, as he was dressing.

"Oh, yes, Mr. Calhoun," Rusty said. She was desperate for him to leave so she could clean herself.

Calhoun walked to the door and left some money on the dresser, which he knew Rusty would give to Lillian.

"I hope you liked it, too, Mr. Calhoun," she said.

"Oh, I did, Rusty," he said. In fact, he was feeling very relaxed and ready to go back home and face his problems.

When he left the room Rusty hurried to the pitcher and basin in the corner and washed herself off.

• • •

Calhoun came out of the building across the street, down the steps, and started walking back in the direction of his house. Clint shook his head. The man had been inside all of fifteen minutes.

EIGHTEEN

Clint watched Calhoun go back into his building then crossed the street to join Rucker once again.

"Anyone else show up?"

"Not yet," Rucker said. "Where'd you go? You weren't gone that long."

Clint explained to Rucker where Calhoun had gone, and how long he'd been inside.

"You're kidding," Rucker said. "Fifteen minutes?"

"That was it."

"Where was this place?"

Clint remembered the street sign and told Rucker where the house was.

"That's Lillian's."

"What's Lillian's?" Clint asked.

"Only the most expensive whorehouse in town."

"What makes it so expensive?"

"She's got beautiful girls there, Clint," Rucker said. "All shapes, sizes, and colors, and all expensive."

71

"Sounds like you've been there."

"Not as a customer," Rucker said. "I couldn't afford that. Some of my colleagues have been there, though."

"As customers?"

"Oh, yeah, and they've told me about it."

"Makes you wish you had more money to spend, huh?"

"I guess it's my curse to be honest."

"That's no curse, Mike."

"Maybe not," Rucker said, "but just once . . ."

He trailed off, but Clint knew what he meant. Just once the young man wished he had enough money to go to Lillian's as a customer.

There were things Clint would have liked to do just once, but going to a whorehouse wasn't one of them, no matter how beautiful the girls, no matter how expensive.

When Calhoun got inside he asked Leo, "Anybody show up?"

"You weren't gone that long, boss."

Calhoun didn't reply to that. He went into his office and went around behind his desk. There was still a pleasant tingle in his loins, and his legs felt slightly shaky. Rusty was no Tanya, but she had done a nice job on him and he was relaxed.

Outside the office Leo shook his head. He marveled at how soon Calhoun came back each time he went to Lillian's. If he had enough money to frequent the most expensive whorehouse in Denver, with the most beautiful women, he'd stay there all day.

A knock at the door broke into his reverie, and he went to answer it.

"Here we go," Rucker said, calling for Clint's attention. "Three men, on foot."

Clint saw them. They were coming from the same direction he and Calhoun had come just a few minutes earlier.

"Recognize any of them?" Clint asked.

"Oh, yeah," Rucker said. "I know all three, I just didn't know they were working for Calhoun."

Rucker described the men to Clint.

Sam Colvin, Matt Bell, and Ed Cook were three of a kind, young men who made their way with a gun but who weren't gunmen.

"They'd never face a man head-on," Rucker said. "That's what makes them perfect for Calhoun and his League."

They watched the three men, all in their late twenties, enter Calhoun's home, admitted by the man who had admitted Clint earlier.

"Who's that letting them in?"

"That's Leo Horton," Rucker said. "He works for Calhoun, inside and outside. Sort of a right-hand man."

Leo showed the three young men into Calhoun's office. This was the team Calhoun considered to be his second best one. They were young, and eager, and they did what they were told. What kept them from the best was that they had no initiative. They could do what they were told, all right, but if things went wrong there wasn't one of them who would take control and make a decision. Calhoun had been thinking about splitting them up.

"You wanted to see us, boss?" Colvin, the unofficial leader of the three, asked.

Calhoun eyed the three young men for a few moments, then asked them the same questions he'd asked Hedge and the others.

"Boss," Colvin said, "I can speak for all of us when I say I don't know what the hell you're talkin' about. We ain't seen Clint Adams at all. We didn't even know he was in Denver."

"I hope you're not lying to me, Sam," Calhoun said. "If you went after him out of some misplaced sense of loyalty I can forgive that. If you lie to me, however, that I can't forgive."

"I'm tellin' you the truth, boss," Colvin said, and the other two men nodded their agreement.

"All right, then," Calhoun said, "you can go."

"You, uh, got any work for us, boss?" Colvin asked.

"Maybe by the end of the month, Sam," Calhoun said. "I've got to get some things cleared up, first. The three of you just stay out of trouble, you hear?"

"We hear ya, boss," Colvin said.

As they left Leo stepped into the room.

"You believe 'em?"

"Yes, I do," Calhoun said. "None of them are smart enough to lie."

"You want some food while you're waitin' for the others, boss?"

"Sure, Leo," Calhoun said, "that sounds good. I worked up an appetite at Lillian's."

Leo didn't know how his boss could have worked up an appetite in that short a time, but he was smart enough to keep his mouth shut about that.

NINETEEN

"Something bothers me about this," Clint said.

"What?" Rucker asked.

"Well, the Calhoun I knew wouldn't have been smart enough to put this thing together."

"You think there's somebody else behind it?" Rucker asked. "Somebody he reports to?"

"Maybe," Clint said. "I just don't see how he could have gotten this much smarter since I last saw him."

"So who do you think's behind it?"

"I wouldn't be able to guess at that," Clint said. "This is your city, not mine."

Rucker frowned.

"I couldn't guess at this point."

"Give it some thought," Clint said, keeping his eyes on Calhoun's front door. "Maybe something will come to you before we're done here today."

"You know," Rucker said, "there's really no point in you staying here all day. All I'm going to do is take a look at these men so I'll know them again. I don't need you for that.''

"I don't have anything else to do," Clint said. "I've already talked to Roper."

"We haven't really had a chance to talk about that," Rucker said. Clint had told him when they met at the Denver House that he spoke with the private investigator, but they hadn't discussed particulars.

"There's not much to talk about, really," Clint said. "He agreed to help. Now all we need to do is figure out what we want him to do."

"Maybe he could look into the possibility of Calhoun fronting for somebody," Rucker said. "He would have the contacts in high places to find that out."

"You're right about that," Clint said. "Roper seems to be able to operate at any level of society, from your street people all the way up to politicians."

"Three more," Rucker suddenly announced.

"You know," Clint said, "this is actually an indication that Calhoun is not as smart as he wants people to think."

"What do you mean?"

"Well, having these men come to see him by threes, that could attract a lot of attention. It would have been smarter to go and meet them somewhere, and maybe meet one man to represent all three."

"You've got a point," Rucker said. "Maybe you're right about there being someone else pulling his strings."

"And this is his way of taking a power trip," Clint

said, "having all these men come to see him. Do you know these three?"

"One of 'em," Rucker said, "but that one is bad enough."

"What do you mean?"

"It's Johnny Dancer."

"Dancer?" Clint said. "I thought he was dead."

"So did I."

As he approached the door with Terry Hogan and Marv Davis in tow, Johnny Dancer was thinking the same thing that Rucker and Clint were. This was not a smart thing to do. He should have insisted on meeting Calhoun someplace out of the way.

He stopped at the door and looked around. Dancer had the feeling he was being watched, and he didn't like that feeling. He knew that the word had gone out that he was dead, and he had intended to use that to get a rest. How he'd ended up working for Lyle Calhoun he didn't know. Yes, he did, it was the money. He'd never been the type to save money; it always seemed to slip through his fingers. When the word went out that he was dead, if he'd had money, he really could have disappeared. But instead he found himself working for Calhoun, shooting men in the back for money. Wanted men, sure, but still men. How had he sunk this low?

When the door opened he looked into the eyes of Leo Horton.

"Hello, Johnny."

"Leo."

"Boys," Leo said to the other two behind Dancer. "Come on in, the boss is waiting for you."

The boss, Dancer thought, shaking his head as he entered. Did he ever think that he would have fallen this far, that he'd be calling somebody like Lyle Calhoun his boss?

Not for a minute, and yet here he was.

"He's in the office," Leo said, "I'll show you—"

"I know the way, Leo," Dancer said. "Come on, boys."

Dancer led the way down the hall to Calhoun's office. The "boss" looked up from his desk as the three men entered the room.

"Where's Leo?"

"I told him to get lost," Dancer said. "What'd you bring us here for, Calhoun?"

Calhoun stared at Dancer. When he hired the man he knew he was taking a big chance. He was supposed to be in charge, but a man like Dancer still scared him. Luckily, Dancer needed the money, and that was Calhoun's edge, but he was never sure what the man was going to do, or how he was going to react when they met. He would have let him go, but Dancer, Hogan, and Davis were his biggest moneymakers.

"I've got a question to ask you boys . . ."

TWENTY

"What makes you think," Johnny Dancer asked, "that I'd try to back-shoot a man like Clint Adams?"

"Seems to me that'd be the only way to kill 'im," Marv Davis said, snickering. He was cut off when Dancer backhanded him across the mouth. The blow staggered the younger, slighter man across the room but didn't knock him down.

"What'd you do that for?"

"A man like Clint Adams deserves better than getting back-shot by the likes of you!" Dancer snapped.

"Geez," Davis said, looking at the blood on his hand from his split lip, "what is he, your brother?"

"I have more in common with him than I'll ever have with you," Dancer said. He turned his attention back to Calhoun, who by now had his hand on the gun in his desk drawer, just in case.

"Are you sending somebody after Adams?" he demanded. "There's no price on his head."

"No," Calhoun said, "there isn't, and that's my

point. I don't want anybody going after him on my account.''

"You got a beef with him, that's your business," Dancer said, "it's got nothing to do with our arrangement.''

"I agree wholeheartedly.''

"Is he in Denver?''

"Yes," Calhoun said, relaxing his hand and removing it from the gun, now that he thought it was safe to do so. "Do you know him?''

"Never met him," Dancer said, "but I've got a lot of respect for him.''

"That's obvious," Davis said, but Dancer let it pass and ignored it.

Standing on the other side of him, Terry Hogan maintained his silence. He didn't want to take a chance on saying something that might get him hit in the mouth.

"Is that all you wanted us for?" Dancer asked. "To ask if we were trying to do you a favor?''

"That's it.''

"This was silly, Calhoun," Dancer said, "making us come here. Next time you want to talk to all three of us let's meet somewhere neutral.''

"Sure, Johnny," Calhoun said, "that's a sound suggestion.''

"We'd better go and take care of Marv's lip," Dancer said.

"See you, Johnny, boys.''

"Mmph," Davis said, with his hand over his mouth. Terry Hogan just waved.

They walked to the front door where they encountered Leo Horton again. He was admitting three more men. This was even more stupidity, Dancer thought, not staggering the meeting times. Now there was a goddamned crowd in the place.

"Hey, Marv," Harry Burke said with a smile, "what happened to your mouth?"

"Don't ask," Davis said and stepped outside with Hogan.

"Leo," Burke said, "why don't you take Frank and Jerry back to the office. I want to talk to Johnny."

"Sure, Harry."

"What's on your mind, Burke?" Dancer asked. He didn't like Harry Burke, and the feeling was mutual.

"I just thought maybe I'd get some tips from the first team is all," Burke said.

"You don't need any tips on shooting men in the back, Harry," Dancer said. "You've been doing business that way for years."

Dancer's remark didn't faze Burke at all.

"Oh, that's right, Johnny," he said, "you're new to this game, ain'tcha? Wonder why Calhoun thinks you're the best at it, though. Maybe because . . . it came so naturally to ya? Do ya think?"

"I do think, Harry," Dancer said, "which is something you'll never be accused of—and I'll leave before you can come up with an answer, because that could take forever and I don't have that much time."

With that Dancer left, closing the door behind him, blocking out Harry Burke's dark glare.

•   •   •

"Harry Burke," Rucker said, "and Johnny Dancer."

"That's not a match made in heaven," Clint said. "Those two don't like each other at all."

"Doesn't look like they're working together, though."

"You know what, Mike? I think I'll trail Johnny and see where he's staying."

"You gonna talk to him?"

"Maybe," Clint said. "I can't see a man like him working for Lyle Calhoun, shooting other men in the back."

"Wanted men."

"It doesn't matter," Clint said. "Johnny Dancer's fallen a long way if he's taking money from Calhoun to back-shoot wanted men. I think I'd like to find out why."

"Well, be careful," Rucker said as Clint stepped out of their shared doorway. "I don't know who those other two are, or how they'll react if they spot you."

"Don't worry," Clint said. "I'm always careful. Why don't we meet back at my hotel. Burke and his buddies should be the last threesome, right?"

"Right," Rucker said. "Your hotel, one hour?"

"See you there," Clint said, and started after Johnny Dancer and his two friends.

TWENTY-ONE

"Let's find a saloon, Johnny," Marv Davis said. "I got to soak my lip in alcohol."

"You and Terry go ahead," Dancer said. "I'm going back to my hotel."

"You know," Terry Hogan said, speaking for the first time since they had arrived at Calhoun's house, "with the money we make you could afford to stay in a better hotel."

"The one I'm in suits me," Dancer said. "You boys go ahead. I'll see you later."

"Come on, Marv," Hogan said, "let's get that lip taken care of."

"Marv," Dancer said.

"Yeah?"

"Sorry about the lip."

"Forget it, Johnny," Davis said. "I shoulda kept my mouth shut."

Davis and Hogan went one way, and Johnny Dancer went his own.

• • •

Clint watched as the three men stopped on a street corner, talked for a while, and then separated, with Dancer going on his own. He continued to follow Dancer into a run-down part of town. It became obvious this was where Dancer was staying. The man stopped in front of a hotel with a broken sign that said HOT instead of HOTEL. Instead of going in, however, Dancer crossed the street to a saloon and went inside. This saloon was more like a Western saloon than any other Clint had seen since arriving in Denver. In fact, the whole neighborhood was more like Dodge City than Denver.

Clint crossed the street and impulsively entered the saloon. He stood inside the door for a moment, attracting some attention but not much. He looked around and saw Dancer standing at the end of the bar with a beer in front of him. Clint walked to the opposite end and also ordered a beer.

"How much do I owe you?" he asked as the bartender set the beer down in front of him.

"Nothin'."

"What did I do to deserve a beer on the house?"

"It ain't on the house," the bartender said. "Fella at the end of the bar sent it to you. Wants to know if you'll join him at a table."

Clint looked down at the end of the bar, and Johnny Dancer lifted his beer mug in a silent salute.

"Tell the man I'd be happy to," he said to the barkeep, then said, "Never mind. I'll tell him myself."

Clint took his beer and walked to the other end of the bar.

"There's a table in the back," Dancer said, and they both walked to it. There was an awkward moment when both wanted to sit with their backs to the wall. Finally, Dancer moved aside and sat adjacent to that chair, which Clint took. From here they could both see the door, and Dancer could still see most of the room.

"Guess I'll have to depend on you to watch my back," Dancer said.

"When did you spot me?" Clint asked. "From the beginning?"

"I don't think so," Dancer said. "I don't know where the beginning was, unless it was at Calhoun's."

"It was."

"I spotted you when I split up from the others."

"Is that hotel across the street really where you're staying?"

"It is. It's more my style than these fancy places. I'll bet you're at the Denver House."

"You'd win that bet."

"Are you watching Calhoun, or me?"

"Calhoun."

"You are Clint Adams, right?"

"Right," Clint said, "and you're Johnny Dancer."

"That's right."

"I know your reputation, Johnny."

"Reps are blown up, you know that."

"Yes, I do," Clint said, "but I've heard about you

from people I trust. What are you doing working for someone like Lyle Calhoun?''

Dancer made a face at the mention of Calhoun and tightened his hand around his beer.

''This is where the money is, for now.''

''You need money that bad?''

''I do.''

''There are other jobs.''

''None that pay like this.''

''But Calhoun—''

''He's just the source of the money,'' Dancer said.

''Is he?''

''What do you mean?''

''I mean he's not smart enough to think up the operation he's running.''

''I don't know what you're talking about.''

''I've been told he calls it his Ambush League.''

Dancer smiled at that.

''Does he? How come I never heard that?''

''Maybe because you and he aren't friends.''

''You can say that again.''

''Then why work for him?''

''I told you,'' Dancer said, ''for the money.''

''This is a long fall for the Johnny Dancer I've heard about.''

''Haven't you heard, then?'' Dancer asked. ''That Johnny Dancer's dead.''

TWENTY-TWO

"The only one who can kill that Johnny Dancer is you, Johnny," Clint said.

"Well, I did."

"When?"

"When I agreed to work for Calhoun."

"You can change your mind."

"Can't change what I've done."

"Maybe—"

"What do you care, anyway?"

Clint looked into Johnny Dancer's face. He was about ten years younger than Clint was, but already he had that look in his eyes.

"Maybe I think I could've gone the way you're going," Clint said.

"Yeah, but you didn't," Dancer said. "I used to hear about you all the time."

"Please," Clint said, "don't tell me you always wanted to be like me."

"No," Dancer said, "I wanted to be better than you."

"You still have time."

"To be faster than you, maybe," Dancer said, "but not better. That time's past."

"It's not past if you don't let it be—"

"Forget it, will ya?" Dancer said. "About the only thing left to prove is am I faster than you. I never thought I'd get that chance, but here you are."

Clint sat back.

"This isn't about that, Johnny," Clint said. "This is not about who's faster or who's better."

"I know what it's about," Dancer said. "You want to know who tried to ambush you, who tried to put a bullet in your back. Well, it wasn't me."

"What about—"

"It wasn't Hogan or Davis, either, the other two who were with me. We don't know anything about it."

"I believe you, Johnny."

"You'd better," Dancer said, "because if you go after them you have to go through me. I'm responsible for them."

"Why's that?"

"Because I brought them into this," Dancer said. "See, just the way I always wanted to be better than you, they want to be better than me. Well, I killed that chance for them, too, didn't I?"

Clint sat back, drank half his beer, then set the mug down on the table.

"There's a lot self-pity here, isn't there?"

"Loads of it," Dancer said, "but if you're gonna offer me a way out, forget it."

"You don't want a way out?"

"It's too late."

"I don't think so."

"I do," Dancer said.

"Look," Clint said, "I'm working with an honest policeman who wants to put Calhoun away."

"Forget it."

"Why?"

"Because I work for Calhoun," Dancer said. "Maybe I've sunk low, but I still have some loyalty."

"To Calhoun?"

"To whoever I happen to be working for at the time. I'm not about to turn on him and stab him in the back."

"Of course not," Clint said, "not while you're shooting men in the back for him."

Dancer gave Clint a long, cold stare and sat back in his chair.

"I think this conversation is over, Adams."

"I thought I could talk some sense into you."

"Well," Dancer said, "maybe you just went about it the wrong way, huh?"

"Maybe I did." Clint stood up.

"Don't get in my way, Adams," Dancer said, "or we'll find out the answer to the question I was asking before."

"I'm taking Calhoun down, Johnny," Clint said, "and if you're around him when I do, you'll go down with him. That's not a threat, that's a promise.''

Clint left the saloon without turning his back on the man. After all, Johnny Dancer was now a self-professed back-shooter, wasn't he?

TWENTY-THREE

It had been a bad idea to brace Johnny Dancer, especially since he didn't know the man personally. In fact, it had been arrogant to think he could talk a stranger out of anything. The man was wallowing so deep in self-pity there was no pulling him out. And if he pressed the issue he'd end up killing him in a gunfight.

When he got back to the hotel he found Detective Rucker in the bar, sitting at a table with a beer and a girl.

"Clint, this is Nina."

"Hello," she said.

Nina had a glass of beer in front of her, also. Clint sat down without bothering to get one. She was a small girl with long dark hair and a slender body. She could have been anything from sixteen to twenty-six.

"Nina is one of those other resources I was telling you about," Rucker said.

Clint was surprised. He thought that all of those

other resources were street people. Nina obviously was not.

"She works at Lillian's."

"Oh," Clint said, "the, uh—"

"Whorehouse," she said. "I'm not ashamed of it."

"And there's nothing to be ashamed of," Clint said. "I guess my question is, what is she doing here?"

"I forgot we had a meeting today," Rucker said, "so I brought her along. She said Calhoun was at Lillian's today, but I told her we knew that because you followed him."

"You should have come in," she said to Clint. "We weren't very busy at that time."

"I'm afraid I was," Clint said. "I was following Calhoun and he wasn't there very long."

"He never is," Nina said, "but he pays well so Lillian makes us all make a fuss over him like he was a great lover, or something."

"Have you ever, uh—"

"No," Nina said, "thank God. I think he's . . . foul. Lillian forces me to flirt with him, and offer myself to him, but thank God I'm not his type."

"Who is?"

"Tanya," she said.

"Why Tanya?"

"Because she's got big breasts and a big butt and can look sixteen."

"So can you," Clint said.

Nina smiled and said, "But I'm not fat, like some people."

"Oh."

"What happened with Dancer?" Rucker asked.

Clint gave Nina a pointed look.

"Nina, I think we're finished," Rucker said. "We can meet again later in the week."

"All right," she said, taking no offense at being dismissed. She stood up and looked at Clint. "Come by sometime. Ask for me."

"If I come by," Clint said, "I will." She was very attractive, but there wasn't much chance of his stopping by Lillian's as a customer.

"Bye, Mike."

"Bye."

She flounced off and left the bar, both Clint and Rucker watching her until she was gone.

"Pretty girl," Clint said.

"Yeah."

"You and she, uh—"

"No," Rucker said, "not a chance. She likes older men."

"How much older?"

"Oh, about your age."

"Thanks."

"What happened with Dancer?"

"I think I made a mistake," Clint said, and went on to tell Rucker about it.

"What made you speak to him in the first place?" Rucker asked when he finished his story.

"I thought I might be able to get him over to our side," Clint said, "then we'd have a man inside Calhoun's organization."

"If it is *his* organization."

"That's right," Clint said. "I've got to talk to Roper about that."

"Can you get to him today?"

"Maybe," Clint said. "He wanted to have a steak with me while I'm here. Maybe I can get him to do it tonight."

"I've got to check up on those other jobs I was supposed to be doing today," Rucker said, "and I want to make a list of the men we saw going into Calhoun's today."

"We can get together in the morning for breakfast," Clint said. "Pick a place."

Rucker thought a moment then named a place and gave Clint directions. It was only a few blocks from the Denver House.

"I might be moving to a different hotel," Clint said.

"Did you tell Dancer where you were staying?"

"He guessed."

"You think he'll tell Calhoun?"

"I don't know that he'll even tell Calhoun we spoke," Clint said.

"Why wouldn't he?" Rucker asked. "He works for the man, doesn't he?"

"Yeah, he does, but he's not happy about it."

"Well," Rucker said, standing up, "if you need a suggestion for another hotel let me know."

"I will," Clint said. "I'll make up my mind tonight about staying or moving."

"Well," Rucker said, "I've got a lot to do tonight

before I turn in. I'll see you in the morning at nine.''

"Nine it is."

Rucker left and Clint stayed to finish his beer. It was early to turn in, but he'd been out all day and thought he'd go back to his room to freshen up, and then decide what he was going to do. He probably didn't have enough time to get Roper to go to dinner with him. He should have asked Rucker to send him one of his street people to take Roper the message.

He finished his beer and walked out to the lobby. He paused just in the doorway to look the lobby over. It was huge, and there was usually a lot of traffic, sometimes people just standing around. It'd be hard to notice if someone was watching you, unless you recognized them, and he didn't see any familiar faces. Satisfied that there was no one in the lobby who meant him harm, he walked past the desk to the stairs and up to the second floor.

He walked down the hall to the room and took his key from his pocket. He stopped in front of his door and paused a moment. Clint had a keen sixth sense that usually alerted him to trouble, and he had the distinct impression that there was someone in his room who didn't belong there.

He fitted the key into the lock as quietly as he could, drew his gun, and opened the door.

TWENTY-FOUR

Calhoun paced his office.

He'd questioned all the men who worked for him and they all denied trying to ambush Clint Adams, and yet he felt that three of them had done it. If he had to bet money on one of them it would be Burke. He was always trying to impress Calhoun so he'd elevate him above Dancer's stature. There was little to separate the two men, except that Dancer was smarter and had more self-control. It was for that reason Calhoun was certain Dancer wasn't the one. He didn't care if he impressed Calhoun or not.

Leo came in and saw his boss pacing.

"Anything I can do, boss?"

Calhoun looked at Leo, standing in the doorway, and then said, "Come on in, Leo."

Leo entered.

"Have some brandy."

"Really?"

"Sure."

Leo hurried to the desk and poured himself a glass before Calhoun could change his mind.

"What did you think today, Leo?"

"About what?"

"About the men."

"What about them?"

Calhoun tried to be patient.

"Which one of them do you think would try to ambush Clint Adams in order to impress me?"

"Oh, that's easy," Leo said. "Burke."

"That's what I was thinking."

"He doesn't like Dancer, wants to prove he's better than him. Killing Clint Adams would do that, and it would also get rid of him for you."

"Leo," Calhoun said, "I don't know how you did it, but you seem to be smarter than you look."

"Thanks, boss . . . I think."

"Finish your drink and have the cook prepare dinner for me."

"You eatin' alone?"

"Yes."

Leo downed the rest of his brandy, gave the decanter a last longing look, then left the room, licking the brandy from his lips.

Burke. Next to Dancer, Burke scared Calhoun the most. He tried not to show it to either man, but he thought Dancer knew it. Maybe not Burke. If he did maybe he wouldn't be trying to impress him.

Calhoun sat behind his desk and wondered if it was time to call in his silent partner.

TWENTY-FIVE

The girl sat up in bed and stared at Clint wide-eyed. The lamp on the wall was turned up just enough to bathe the room in a soft yellow light. Clint had gone through this many times before. He was attracted to women, and he attracted them, and sometimes they came to his room. Every once in a while one would come to try to shoot him or stab him, but that was the exception.

For a moment her name eluded him, and then he said, "Amy?"

"You remembered," she said, pleased. Then she frowned. "You scared the hell out of me."

She was holding the sheet up to her neck, but it was molding itself to her so that he could see she was naked. Her nipples made little hills under the sheet.

"What are you doing here?" he asked, holstering his gun and closing the door. "And how did you get in?"

99

"Getting in was easy," she said. "The clerk was susceptible to my charms."

What man wouldn't be, he wondered. She had an extremely pretty face, blond hair, a curvaceous body, and a little girl voice.

"Why am I here is, I think, obvious?" she said, looking down at herself.

"Does Roper know you're here?" Clint was wondering if this was one of Roper's jokes.

"Why does he have to know what I do when I'm on my own time?"

"I thought he might have sent you with a message."

"No, I came on my own."

"Why?"

"I sensed something in you when we met."

"And what was that?"

"Tension."

"Tension?"

"Uh-huh," she said with a nod. "I can help you with that."

"With my tension."

"I can relax you."

He was anything but relaxed at the moment. This naked young woman was having an effect on him—probably her desired effect. He was torn between asking her to leave and pulling the sheet off the bed.

"It won't do any good to ask me to leave," she said, as if reading his mind. "You need me."

"How old are you?"

"That doesn't matter, either," she said, shaking her

head. Her blond curls went on shaking after her head stopped. "I'm old beyond my years."

"Amy, look—"

"No," she said, tossing the sheet away, "you look."

And he did. She was about as pleasingly plump as you could get, much more so than she'd looked when she was dressed. Her breasts were full and round, and her thighs matched. She had a little extra flesh everywhere, but not so that any man would ever complain.

"Are you just gonna stand there and look? You can touch me, you know."

"Amy . . ." he said, shaking his head.

"I know," she said, holding out her arms, "you can't resist me."

He walked to the bed and sat on it. She immediately put her arms around him and pulled him to her for a kiss which went on for a long time. She smelled wonderful, a mixture of perfume, sex, and her own personal scent. Her flesh was so warm he could feel the heat coming off her even before he put his hand on her. She was extremely sensitive; when his hands touched her she shivered, and her nipples tightened.

He broke the kiss, took her breasts in his hands and leaned over to kiss them. She closed her eyes for a moment, then opened them and started to undress him. He helped her, leaving the bed only to kick off his boots and discard his trousers, and then joining her again.

This time she touched him, running her hands over

his chest and belly, then taking his penis gently in her hands and stroking it.

"Lie back," she said. "Trust me. I know how to make you feel good."

And she did. She placed his penis between her pillowy breasts and rolled it there, then released it only to capture it again with her hot mouth. She sucked him expertly, wetly, slurping as if he was some sweet confection that she was devouring. She caressed his balls with one hand while holding his penis with the other, continuing to bob her head up and down, her curls bouncing also. He reached down and put his hands on her shoulders, first simply to touch her and then to push her off him.

"Wha—" she said.

"You're too good at that," he said. "Come up here and lie down so I can return the favor."

"But I want to make you feel good."

"I know," he said, "but part of that is letting me make you feel good."

She stared up at him, apparently puzzled by this concept.

"It's the woman's job—" she started, but he stopped her.

"There's no job here, Amy," he said. "A man and woman in bed are partners, and they have to make each other enjoy every moment."

She moved up alongside him and lay down, still looking puzzled.

"You're the first man who's ever told me that," she said.

"You lie back," he said, sliding one hand down over her belly and finding her wet. He slid his finger along her wetness, and she gasped and jumped. He continued to stroke her while kissing her breasts and sucking her nipples, and before long her belly began to tremble and then she was rolling on the bed, riding the waves of pleasure his touch had given her.

"God . . . God . . ." she said, her eyes closed tight, "what's . . . happening . . ."

It was clear to him that she was feeling something she'd never felt before.

This was going to be fun. . . .

TWENTY-SIX

"Oh, my God," she said later. "I thought I knew all about sex, but . . ."

"Amy, you know a lot about pleasing a man," he said, stroking her body, "but you really don't know that much about sex."

"Well, I never had any complaints before," she said, "but I believe you're right, Clint. I mean . . . where did you learn all that?"

"It's not something you learn," he said, rubbing his palm over her belly, "it's something you feel."

"Well, I was sure feeling it. In fact," she said, as his hand dipped lower, "I'm still feeling it . . ."

"Do you have to be anywhere tonight?"

"No!" she gasped.

"Good," he said, kissing her shoulders, then her neck, still moving his hand through the tangle of blond curls, finding the wetness and then starting again. . . .

* * *

"Stop, stop," she said later.

He was down between her legs, enjoying the scent and taste of her, when she reached down and pushed his head away.

"What is it?"

"You're gonna kill me," she said.

"I wouldn't want to do that," he said, sitting up between her legs. "Are you hungry?"

"God, yes," she said. "You sure know how to make a girl build up an appetite."

"Let's get dressed and I'll buy you a steak in the hotel dining room. Have you ever eaten here?"

"No."

"You'll like it."

She sat up and drew her knees up to his chest.

"Can we have champagne? I love champagne, but I never get to have it."

"Steak and champagne it is," he said, "and then we'll come back up here."

"See?" she said, reaching out and touching his shoulder.

"See what?"

"You needed me," she said. "You're all relaxed now."

"So are you."

"Well," she said, "I didn't know when I got here that I needed you, too. All my muscles feel like liquid."

"Well," he said, starting to dress, "they'll solidify when we get some food."

TWENTY-SEVEN

Over dinner she explained how she had come to be in Denver and working for Talbot Roper.

"I came here from St. Louis," she said, "and my cousin was working for him. I had a couple of jobs here and there, but then she left him to get married and got me the job."

"He's had lots of girls working for him."

"That's what she said," Amy replied. "I intend to be his girl for a while, though. I like the job."

"Do you like him?"

"Oh, yes, he's a very good boss," she said, "and he's never tried to kiss me or anything."

"Your other bosses have?"

"Yes, all of them," she said. "It's really very frustrating to try to work for someone while he's chasing you around his desk."

"I guess it would be."

"And I'm very good at my job," she said. "I keep his office running smoothly, the filing is in order, I make coffee . . . I think I can be there for a long time.''

''Well,'' he said, ''that will be a challenge.''

''Remember when you asked me if he sent me with a message?''

''Did he?''

''No, but he was going to tomorrow,'' she said. ''That's what gave me the idea of coming over tonight.''

''What's the message going to be tomorrow?''

''He wants you to have dinner with him.''

''Well, tell him I will.''

''I can't do that.''

''Why not?''

''Then he'll know we were together tonight.''

''Oh.''

''I'll just let him send me over here tomorrow afternoon,'' she said. ''Will you be here?''

''I don't know.''

''It doesn't matter if you're not,'' she said. ''I can tell him I delivered the message, but if you are here we could, well . . .''

''Yes,'' he said, ''we could, couldn't we? Would you like some more champagne?''

They took a bottle of champagne up to the room with them and drank it in between making love.

''Oooh, God,'' she said at one point, lying on her back and extending her arms and legs, ''you sure do exhaust a girl, Mr. Adams.''

''Is that a complaint?'' he asked.

"Not at all."

He picked the champagne bottle up off the floor and shook it.

"Champagne's gone. Should I get more?"

"No," she said. "My head is spinning. Another bottle will knock me out for the night."

He sprawled beside her and kissed her belly.

"We wouldn't want that, would we?" he asked. "We still have lots to do."

"More?" she asked.

"Unless you'd rather go to sleep?"

She looked down at him and asked, "Could we? Just for a little while?"

He laughed and said, "Sure. To tell you the truth, I'm a little tired myself."

"Oh, I'm glad to hear that," she said.

He pulled the sheet back on the bed, lay down next to her, and let her snuggle close. He started to say something to her but realized that she had fallen asleep in seconds.

And he was only seconds behind her.

TWENTY-EIGHT

They woke and made love once more during the night, but then slept on until the sun streamed in the window and woke them.

"Mmm," she said, stretching her arms over her head, lifting her breasts, pointing her toes. Clint thought that if he were a painter that picture would have sold for a lot of money.

He gathered her into his arms and kissed her a sound good morning.

"Breakfast?" he asked.

"I'm famished."

He put his hand on her belly, but she rolled away from him and hopped off the bed.

"No," she said. "If you start that I'll never want to leave, and I have to go to work."

"So Talbot Roper can send you back here with a message for me."

"That's right."

"I just remembered," he said.

"What?"

"I have to have breakfast with a policeman this morning."

"Well, that's fine, then," Amy said. "That will work out great. You go and have your breakfast. I'll have to go home and get some fresh clothes so Mr. Roper doesn't think I slept in these. After lunch I'll come over and bring you his message."

"And one of your own, I'll bet," he said, making a grab for her.

She jumped back, causing certain body parts to jiggle. He suspected that by the time she reached forty she might have started to put on some more weight, but at the moment, with the sun coming through the window, illuminating her golden hair and the golden down on her arms, she looked as glorious as a woman could look.

"How old did you say you were again?" he asked.

"I didn't," she said. "Now get dressed and get out!"

Clint reached the agreed upon café late, and Rucker was having coffee already.

"Thought you overslept," the detective said.

"No chance of that," he said. "I had a guest over for the evening."

"Ah," Rucker said, "was it Nina? She took a shine to you."

"No," Clint said, sitting down, "not Nina." There was already a second coffee cup on the table, so he poured himself a cup.

"Someone you met last night, then, after I left?"
Rucker asked curiously.

"No," Clint said, "I met her at Talbot Roper's
office."

"Someone looking to hire him?"

"No," Clint said, "she works for him—why are
you so nosy?"

"You brought it up."

"So I did," Clint said, "and now I'm dropping it."

"So I guess you didn't have dinner with Roper last
night," Rucker said.

"No, that will be tonight."

"Good. I've got some things to do today—more
dirty work from the inspector—and I have to do it
myself, so I'll be busy until after dinner. There won't
be much gettin' done today as far as Calhoun's con-
cerned."

"That's fine," Clint said. "I'll have dinner with
Roper and we can catch up afterwards."

"Seems like that's all we do is catch up," Rucker
said. "I've spent more time sitting at tables with you.
I want to get something done!"

"Don't get frustrated, Mike," Clint said. "You're
having an effect already."

"What makes you say that?"

"Has anyone been ambushed lately?" Clint asked.

"Not that we know of."

"All of Calhoun's men are in town," Clint said.
"They're not out plying their trade."

"And you think that's because of me?"

"And me, probably," Clint said. "I don't think

Calhoun wants to take any chances while we're paying attention to him.''

"So what do you think he'll do?"

"I think if he's got a partner," Clint said, "he's going to have to go and talk to him."

"So we've got to tail him again," Rucker said.

"Which may not be as easy this time," Clint said. "We need someone he won't notice."

Rucker smiled and said, "Leave that to me. I know just the little fella to use."

"Little fella?"

"You'll meet him soon enough," Rucker said. "Now let's have breakfast so I can get on with my day, and you with yours. I'm hungry."

"So am I," Clint said. "In fact, I'm starved."

"Sure, you are," Rucker said. "After all, you had company all night."

TWENTY-NINE

Clint was in his room in the afternoon when there was a knock on the door. He opened it and found Amy standing there, smiling broadly. She pushed him into the room, removed all her clothing—and then his—and delivered her message before she delivered her boss's.

"He wants you to meet him at the Cattleman Club," Amy said, as they lay side by side, catching their breath. "Do you know where that is?"

"Yes," Clint said, "I've eaten with him there before."

Suddenly, she bounded up off the bed.

"You make me forget myself," she said. "I have to get back to work."

He was treated to the pleasure of watching her dress, and he enjoyed every moment of it.

"You look like you truly enjoy watching a woman dress," she said.

"I enjoy watching you dress," he said. "Not as

113

much as I enjoy watching you undress, but I enjoy it.''

Fully dressed she walked to the bed and kissed him.

"When will I see you again?" she asked.

"I don't know," he said. "I don't know when I'll get back tonight, but then, you didn't have any trouble getting into my room before."

"You won't mind if I'm here waiting for you?"

"I can't think why I would mind," he said, pulling her down by her arm and kissing her again. She melted into the kiss for a moment, then pulled away from him and ran for the door.

"You're gonna get me fired," she said and ran out.

Later that evening he went to meet Talbot Roper at the Cattleman Club, a gentlemen's social club that counted among its members some of the wealthiest men in Denver—and Talbot Roper.

"Can I help you, sir?" He was greeted by a smug-looking man in a monkey suit.

"I'm meeting a friend."

"Is your friend a member, sir?"

"He is."

Clint decided to give the guy a hard time, and didn't elaborate.

The man waited, then cleared his throat and asked, "And what is his name, sir?"

"Talbot Roper."

Suddenly, the man was all smiles and his demeanor changed completely.

"Of course, Mr. Roper's guest," he said expansively. "This way, please, sir. It will be my pleasure to take you to him."

"Thank you."

They walked through a huge foyer. On one side was a room where men were sitting, smoking cigars and discussing the stock market, the price of beef, and who would be the next heavyweight champion of the world. On the other side was the dining room, and this was the room the man took Clint to.

"Here is Mr. Roper," the man said, leading Clint to Roper's table. "Mr. Roper, your guest has arrived."

"Thank you, George."

"Sir?" George said, holding Clint's chair.

"Thank you."

"Enjoy your meal, gentlemen."

"We will, George," Roper said.

"I guess that's George."

"That's him."

"Great personality."

"He's not bad when you get to know him."

"Well, I won't be."

"He rubbed you the wrong way," Roper said. "He can do that."

"He can do that very well," Clint said.

"I'm glad my girl got you my message," he said, tactfully changing the subject. "It took her somewhat longer than I expected."

"She delivered it very well."

"You dog," Roper said, "you've had her."

Clint didn't answer.

"You've had that sweet, plump, luscious body, haven't you?"

"What's good here?"

"You know what's good here, you've eaten here before, answer the question."

"Oh, yes," Clint said, "I remember eating here before *George* worked here."

"George has been here for nine years," Roper said. "He had the day off the last time you came." He leaned close to Clint, looming over the table. "You're not going to tell me, are you?"

"A gentleman," Clint said, "never tells."

"Gentleman!" Roper said, sitting back with a laugh. "When did you become a gentleman?"

"When you became a dirty old man," Clint said. "You want the girl?"

"Of course not," Roper said. "She works for me. I just want to know if you had her. She's so ripe she's about to burst!"

"I think," Clint said, "I'll have the steak. . . ."

THIRTY

"Okay, so let me get this straight," Roper said over coffee and peach pie. "You think Calhoun has a partner?"

"A partner, a boss," Clint said. "Somebody's got to be the brains behind him."

"And you want me to find out who it is."

"It's got to be somebody with money. You know the moneyed people in this city."

"Why somebody with money?"

"I've been thinking about it," Clint said. "What if Calhoun winning all that money was just a scam, a way to set him up in business here?"

"Well," Roper said, "if that were the case I guess I'd have to take a long hard look at who was in that game."

"And that game was held right here in Denver."

"Poker," Roper said, "that's your game."

"But we're not interested in playing in a game," Clint said, "just who was playing in that game."

"That's right."

"And who was running it."

"That, too. Did you have any friends in that game?"

"No," Clint said. "I didn't hear about the game until after it was done, which at the time I thought was odd."

"Because you weren't invited?" Roper asked.

"No," Clint said, "but I didn't know anything about it, and neither did Bat or Luke Short. You think anybody's going to have a big game without them?"

"Then tell me why somebody did."

"Because with them in the game," Clint said, "nobody could cheat."

Roper thought it over a few minutes, then nodded and said, "That makes sense."

"Then you'll do it?"

"Sure," Roper said, "I'll do it because you asked, but also because it sounds interesting."

"And," Clint said, "because you might be able to finger some rich member of this club."

Roper smiled and looked around the dining room. The only reason he had a membership in the club was that somebody paid for it for him—somebody he had done a job for, somebody who was extremely grateful—otherwise he knew he'd never be in that club.

"You know," he said to Clint, "they're still trying to get me out of this club."

"Now, why would they want to go and do a thing like that?"

"They think I'm beneath them."

"So every time you bring one of them in," Clint said, "you show them that you're not."

"Right."

"So here's another chance."

"Right again."

"Talbot, when did you get so vindictive?"

"Did you sleep with my secretary last night?"

"I think I want another piece of this pie."

Later, they left the club together. As they were walking through the foyer to the front door Clint looked into the other room.

"Don't you want to go in there with your fellow members and have a cigar, read the paper, talk some stocks?" he asked his friend.

"If I did that," he said, "several of those men in there would shit a brick."

"That'd be worth seeing," Clint said, and then added, "I guess."

"Come on," Roper said. "The only reason I come here is that the steaks are good, and it annoys most of the members."

"George seems to like you," Clint said. "At least you have a friend in George."

"Come on . . ." Roper said, and headed for the door.

THIRTY-ONE

Over dinner Clint had discussed with Roper whether or not there was a need for him to change hotels, and they both agreed that there was.

"You can't trust Johnny Dancer, not in the shape he's in," Roper said, and Clint realized that was true.

So after dinner he went back to the Denver House to check out, but then he realized that Amy might be in his room. He went up to get his things, and she wasn't there yet. If he left, she wouldn't be able to find him, and he didn't know where she lived to find her to tell her.

He was packing his things when there was a knock at the door. He answered it, thinking it would be Amy. Instead, it was a small boy.

"Are you Adams?" the boy asked.

"Uh, yes, I am."

The boy was filthy—his clothes and him—and appeared to be nine, but he had the demeanor of a forty-year-old.

"Mike Rucker sent me."

Ah, Clint thought, one of Rucker's street people. Then he remembered Rucker had referred to one as the "little fella." This lad certainly lived up to that name.

"For what?"

"To talk to you."

"Why?"

"He had me follow some rich guy today, and I'm supposed to tell you about it." The boy looked past Clint into the room. "You gettin' ready to leave?"

"I was switching hotels."

"Know where you're switchin' to?"

"Not yet," Clint said. "Why don't you come downstairs with me and tell me what happened while I check out."

"Sure," the kid said, "c'mon."

"Hey, what's your name?"

"Spike."

"Sure it is. . . ."

Spike had picked Calhoun up at his house that afternoon around three and followed him.

"He caught a cab in front of his house and I lost 'im right away."

"How did you follow him, then?"

Spike grinned and said, "I know the driver of the cab. I found him, and he took me to where he left Calhoun off."

"And where was that?"

"The bank district," Spike said.

"You must have stuck out there."

"Naw," Spike said, "I go down there all the time for handouts. Those people are real generous."

"Okay," Clint said, as they went down the stairs, "so he went to the banking district. Then what?"

"Well, the driver didn't know which building he went into, so I had to wait and see."

"And?"

"I hung around for an hour before I seen him come out of one of the buildings."

"Which one?"

"The First Denver Bank. Folks around here call it Denver One."

They reached the front desk and suspended the conversation while Clint checked out.

"Hope you enjoyed your stay," the clerk said. It was not the same clerk who had checked him in.

"I did," Clint said, then added, "Oh, and I want to thank you for letting my . . . friend into my room."

The clerk smiled, winked, and said, "My pleasure, sir."

Clint turned and started through the lobby with Spike at his side.

"That dope let someone into your room?"

"Yeah," Clint said, "a woman."

"He should get fired."

"Maybe I'll talk to the management."

When they reached the front door Clint stopped.

"What else happened, Spike?"

"Nothing," Spike said. "The guy went back home."

"Am I supposed to give you some money?"

Spike shrugged.

"Rucker didn't say nothin' about that."

"Play—"

"But you could."

"I tell you what," Clint said. "Do something else for me and I will."

"What do I gotta do?"

"Wait here for my friend to come and tell her where I went."

"A woman?"

"Yeah."

"What's she look like?"

Clint described Amy.

"Wow."

"Will you do that for me?"

"Sure."

Clint handed the kid five dollars.

"Wow!"

"I'll have some more for you later."

"Thanks."

"Tell me something."

"What?"

"If I got into a cab and told the driver to take me to Denver One, would he know what I was talking about?"

"Sure he would," Spike said, "or he shouldn't be driving a cab in Denver."

"Okay, now I need one more favor."

"What's that?:

"Recommend a hotel."

"High-class, medium, or low?"

"Let's go with medium this time."

"I know just the place . . ."

THIRTY-TWO

The hotel Spike recommended was called the Roberts Hotel and it truly was "medium." It was several steps down from the Denver House, but several miles above the hotel Johnny Dancer was staying in. Clint checked in under the name "Jim West," and went to leave his gear in his room. He doubted Amy would have trouble getting the clerk at this hotel to let her into his room.

That done he went back outside and got himself a cab.

"Can you take me to Denver One?"

"Banking hours might be over by the time we get there, friend," the driver said.

"I'll chance it."

"Suit yourself."

"I'll double the fare if they're not over by the time we get there."

"Now you're talkin'," the man said enthusiastically.

He got onto his horse and they pulled up in front of Denver One at ten minutes to five. Clint got out and paid the driver.

"Want me to stick around?"

"No," Clint said, "I don't know when I'll be going back."

"I can come back."

"In half an hour?"

"Sure," the driver said. "I'll pick you up right here."

"Thanks."

"Thank *you*."

The cab pulled away and Clint turned and looked at the First Denver Bank building. It was built of stone and brick and was four stories high. When he went inside he saw that there was construction going on in the lobby. There was also a list on the wall of the companies who had offices in the buildings, as well as a list of men's names. He went over and looked at them, but didn't recognize any of them. He didn't even know what he was doing down here. He should have just given the name of the building to Roper and let him do it. He'd undoubtedly recognize some of the names.

Clint turned and saw a workman walking toward him.

"Hey, what's all the construction for?"

"We're puttin' in one of them elevators," the man said.

Clint had seen elevators in New York but never this far west.

"First one in this city," the man went on. "First one anywhere in the country was in New York, in 1859, in the Fifth Avenue Hotel. Guess it's taken them almost twenty-five years to get this far west."

"Guess so," Clint agreed.

"Folks'll still be takin' the stairs for a while, though," the man said, " 'til they get used to it."

"Thanks for the information."

"Sure."

"Hey?"

"Yeah?"

"When will it be running?"

"Pretty soon, now," the man said. "We're jest puttin' the finishin' touches to 'er."

"Thanks again."

Clint went out of the Denver One building to wait for the cab. As he did he noticed that the buildings around him—and Denver One—were suddenly belching people out onto the street. Banking hours were over, apparently, and that seemed to trigger a mass exodus.

He watched the front door of the Denver One building but didn't recognize anyone who came out. By five-thirty, when the cab returned, all of the buildings seemed to be empty.

"This is like a ghost town now," the cab driver said. "You never woulda got a cab if I didn't come back for ya."

"I'll remember that," Clint said, "when it comes time for me to pay you."

THIRTY-THREE

The driver dropped Clint in front of his hotel, and Clint was generous when he paid him.

"Hey, Spike," the driver yelled, when he saw the boy in front of the hotel.

"Hey, Cal," Spike said. "You take good care of my man, here?"

"This fella's a friend of yours?"

"Sure."

"Mister," the driver said, "you shoulda tole me you was friends with Spike."

He offered Clint the money back that he paid him, both ways, but Clint insisted that he keep it. The man thanked him and drove away.

"What are you doing here, Spike?" Clint asked.

"You told me to let that lady know where you were," the boy reminded him.

"So?"

"I brung her."

"Well . . . that was real nice of you."

"What about Rucker?"

"What about him?"

"You want him to know where you are, too?"

"That would be a good idea. Do you know where he is?"

"Sure I do."

"Okay, then," Clint said, "you let him know."

He handed the boy two more dollars.

"Thanks, mister."

"Call me Clint."

"Okay, Clint." He started away, then turned back. "Hey, about that lady?"

"Yeah?"

"She didn't look nothin' like you said."

"What do you—" Clint started to ask, but Spike was gone.

Clint shook his head and went into the hotel. He walked up to the second floor, down the hall to his room, and opened the door with his key.

"I'm glad you found your way here—" he started, and then stopped when he saw the woman on the bed.

"I'm glad you feel that way," the dark-haired girl said, smiling. "I had the feeling you weren't going to come and see me at Lillian's."

"Hello, Nina."

He closed the door behind him.

"Were you?"

"I don't think so."

"Why not? Don't you find me attractive?"

She was sitting on the bed, fully dressed, and yet she projected sex from every pore.

"I think you're very attractive," he said, "but you seem so young—"

"I'm twenty-five," she said. "I know I look younger, and I can look a lot younger, but I'm twenty-five."

"Well, then, I guess I should tell you that I'm not in the habit of paying for sex."

"I didn't think so," she said. "When you came in you were expecting someone else, weren't you?"

"Uh, well, yes . . ."

"So you already have a friend in town."

"Well, sort of . . ."

She stood up and the fabric of her dress whispered. He instinctively knew she had nothing on underneath.

"So then, you're not interested in me?"

"I didn't say that . . ."

"Am I too small?"

"No," Clint said, "that's not a problem."

She did something behind her back and suddenly the bottom part of her dress fell to the floor. He saw that he was right. She was naked underneath, and now he could see her strong, shapely legs, and the dark pubic thatch between her legs. He could also smell her.

She turned around and walked around the bed, showing him her ass. It was small, but solid and round. She removed the top part of her dress, tossing it away, and he admired the line of her back as it plunged down into the crease between her buttocks. Then she turned and he saw her breasts, small, with large, brown nipples—erotic nipples, which were hardening as he stared at them.

She pulled back the bedclothes to expose the sheets and got onto the bed, remaining on her knees.

"Come on," she said. "You'll enjoy it."

"I know I will."

"So will I," she said, "and I won't charge you a dime."

"Why not?"

"Because you're not some fat cowboy or merchant or banker who's trying to get away from his wife. Because you're interesting."

"Rucker told you about me, didn't he?"

"He did," she said. "So what? What does it matter why I find you attractive or interesting?"

"Nina, look," Clint said, "I'm not sure that, uh, Amy—that's my other friend—"

"You're afraid she'll show up here?"

"It's possible."

"That's okay with me," Nina said with a lascivious smile. "I can handle that, too. . . ."

Suddenly Clint's eyes fastened onto a small beauty mark just to the right of her mouth, which was small, thin-lipped, but very pretty.

"Come on, Clint," she said. "I'm waiting for you. Maybe we can finish before your girlfriend gets here. . . . I wouldn't count on it, though. I intend to enjoy you, and for you to enjoy me."

Clint couldn't help it, then. What man could? By now the room was filled with the heady scent of her.

He walked to the bed, and she moved on her knees

to the edge and began to unbutton his shirt. He leaned
over and kissed that beauty mark, and then her mouth.
Two beautiful young women in two days, how could
one man get so lucky? And why should he turn one
down?

Why, indeed?

THIRTY-FOUR

Nina's mouth was much more than pretty, it was talented. Hours later she was crouched down between his legs using that lovely mouth to bring him to fullness again. She was sucking him, stroking him, cooing to him, making him harder than before, if that was possible. Then she straddled him, closed her eyes, and brought herself down onto him, taking him inside her steamy depths slowly, inch by inch, until he was inserted fully into her.

"Oooh," she said, and began to rotate her hips. He reached for her breasts, popped the large nipples between his fingers, slid his hands around to cup her ass, felt her wetness there, on her cheeks, on his hands, soaking the sheet.

She began to move on him faster and faster then, her eyes closed, seeking her own satisfaction again, even though they had satisfied each other several times by now. It had been a long time since he'd met two girls like Amy and Nina, who enjoyed sex so much. He wondered if it came from living in a city rather than in some small Western town.

She made a noise in her throat, and suddenly he felt her thighs and her belly begin to tremble. He turned her over then, lifting her slight weight easily, shifting her onto her back and taking control.

He got up on his knees, still inside her, grasped her by the ankles, spread her apart and began fucking her hard and fast. She gasped and moaned every time he drove into her, slid her hands down between her legs to touch herself wantonly. He found that very erotic and suddenly found that he had to fight to keep himself from finishing.

She continued to touch herself as he drove into her, and then she touched him, reaching down for his testicles, stroking him, pulling him down onto her so she could reach his ass cheeks, stroked him there, and then slid one finger between them, touching him, urging him on, and then she slipped over the edge and he stopped fighting and went over just behind her. . . .

"Wow."

"That's an appropriate word."

"One I've never used before," she said. "Not to describe sex, anyway."

"Well," Clint said, "it is a job to you, isn't it?"

"Most of the time," she said, "but it sure wasn't tonight."

He was lying on his side and she snuggled up against his back.

"Are you glad I came here?"

"I'd be lying if I said I wasn't."

"Good, because I have a confession to make."

"What's that?"

"Your other friend? What's her name?"

"Amy."

"Yeah, her," Nina said. "I told your little friend, Spike, not to tell her where you were. I mean, I *did* get there first tonight. That should count for something, shouldn't it?"

"So there's no danger of her showing up here?"

"None," Nina said, "unless she finds out from somebody else."

"I don't think that'll happen."

"Not mad?"

He rolled over to face her, kissed her beauty mark and said, "No, I'm not mad."

"Good." She put her hand on his hip, stroked him, then his right buttock, then his leg, his chest . . .

"Can I ask you something?" Clint said.

"Is this about work?"

"Yes."

"You're not gonna ask me why I do it, are you?" she asked.

"No," he said, "it's not that kind of question."

"Okay, then," she said, "go ahead and ask."

"How often does Lyle Calhoun go to Lillian's?"

"A couple of times a week, I guess."

"And does he ever stay longer than he did the other day?"

She made a rude noise with her mouth and said,

"The great lover? No. Everybody laughs at him. We call him the ten-minute wonder."

"It only takes him that long to finish?"

"It only takes him that long to undress, finish, get dressed and leave the money on the dresser. He thinks he's doing the girls a favor. Well, actually, I guess he is."

"How so?"

"They never have to spend more than ten or fifteen minutes with him."

"Ah. What about friends?"

She laughed and slid her hand down between his legs, just to stroke him.

"We have lots of friends."

"No, I mean Calhoun. Does he ever bring friends there?"

"Sometimes," Nina said.

"Like who?"

"Men with money, usually."

"More money than him?"

"Oh, yes," she said, "more money, more stamina, more everything."

"Bankers?"

"Sure."

"Politicians?"

"Some."

"How did Calhoun get to come to Lillian's?"

"Somebody brought him."

"Like who?"

She frowned.

"I think that was a banker. Oh, yeah, I remember

now. His name is Charles Belmont the third.''

''The third?''

''Oh, yes,'' she said, affecting a mock tone of seriousness, ''you have to say the third, or else it could be his father or grandfather.''

''How old is this Belmont the third?''

''Oh,'' she closed one eye cutely while thinking, ''I think he's forty or so.''

''And are his father and grandfather still alive?''

''Sure are, and active.''

''Active where?''

''In their bank.''

''And what bank would that be?'' Clint asked, thinking that he already knew.

''The biggest,'' she said. ''They own Denver One.''

Clint smiled. He felt as if he'd just drawn to an inside straight in a big poker game, and filled in.

THIRTY-FIVE

Clint chased Nina out, saying he still had some things to do that evening. Reluctantly, she got out of bed and got dressed. He watched her, thinking how he had watched Amy early that morning, wondering how it was women moved differently even when they dressed.

When she was ready to leave she sat on the bed and regarded him sternly.

"You're gonna have to come and see me now," she said, "because I won't know when your other little friend is here with you."

"I don't think there's much danger of that," Clint said. "She probably thinks I sneaked away on her."

"I wouldn't worry," she said, putting her hand on his chest. "If you did just some of the things to her that you did to me tonight, she'll forgive you."

She leaned over and kissed him.

"Come and see me soon."

"I will."

"I won't charge you," she said, walking to the door. "I promise."

She blew him a kiss from the door and was gone.

Calhoun stared across the huge mahogany desk at Charles Belmont III, his silent partner.

"So this Adams is going to be a problem?" Belmont asked.

"He is a problem," Calhoun said, "and so is the policeman, Rucker."

"Get rid of them, then."

"If we kill a policeman it's going to make things worse," Calhoun said.

"I'll take care of the policeman, then," Belmont said, "you take care of Clint Adams."

"Me? I can't—"

"Have it done, Calhoun," Belmont said. "That's why you have men working for you."

"I've been trying to find out who tried to kill him once already."

"What does that matter?"

"Well . . . he said if someone tries again he's going to come after me."

"Then you'd better make sure that if someone tries again, they succeed. Do you have someone who could do that for you?"

"Burke," Calhoun said, "maybe Burke . . . but Dancer, he could do it."

"Then have both of them do it."

"Work together? Those two? I don't think they would," Calhoun said.

"Offer them enough money," Belmont said with certainty, "and they will."

After Calhoun left, Belmont went to the window of his fourth floor office and looked down at the street. He saw Calhoun appear and get into a cab. He hated it when the man came to the Denver One building, but at least it didn't happen very often.

He turned and went back to his desk. This whole Ambush League had been a game to him, a lark, something to relieve the monotony of the banking business. Now it was threatening to blow up in his face. Calhoun was on the verge of panicking, even if he didn't know it himself. If Calhoun didn't manage to get rid of Clint Adams, Belmont knew he was going to have to get rid of Calhoun. If his father and grandfather found out what he was up to, they might kick him out of the family business. It might have been boring, but he certainly wasn't looking to give it up.

THIRTY-SIX

Clint still didn't know where Amy lived so he couldn't get to her until tomorrow to explain. That was good, because he needed time to come up with an explanation.

The hotel had a bar, so he sat in there and waited to see if Rucker would show, once Spike gave him the name of the hotel. Surprisingly, it wasn't Rucker who appeared, but Talbot Roper.

"How did you find me?" Clint asked as the man sat across from him.

"A friend of mine told me you were here."

"A friend named Spike?"

"That's the one."

"The little guy gets around."

"Not so little."

"What is he," Clint asked, "nine or ten?"

Roper smiled.

"He's fifteen."

"Come on."

"I'm not lying."

"He's . . . small for his age."

"He uses that in his favor," Roper said.

"I guess so."

"I think I've found your silent partner," Roper said. "A banker."

"Charles Belmont the third."

Roper stopped, stared at Clint, then asked, "If you know these things already, why ask me to find out?"

"I just happened to come across the name."

"During what?"

"Pillow talk."

Roper frowned.

"How would Amy know—"

"It wasn't Amy."

"But you did sleep with her, right?"

"It was a girl named Nina," Clint said, "who works at Lillian's."

"You using whores now?"

"No," Clint said, "I kind of think she used me, and I didn't have to pay."

"How do you do that?"

"Do what?"

"Get to be with a prostitute without paying?"

Clint shrugged and said, "They like me."

"I guess so," Roper said. "Do you want to know what I found out?"

"Sure I do," Clint said, "otherwise I'd just be wasting your time, right?"

"Calhoun's partner is Charles Belmont the third. You know that. Do you also know that the Belmonts own the First Denver Bank, also known as Denver One?''

"No," Clint lied, "I didn't know that.''

"Well, he and his father and his grandfather run this bank, but apparently Charlie Three—that's what his family calls him—got a little bored with banking and decided to branch out. He did a lot of research, Charlie Three did, and came up with Lyle Calhoun to front for him. He put together this phony big-time card game, hired a card sharp to deal, and made sure Calhoun won all the money.''

"So Calhoun could set himself up well here in Denver with his winnings, and nobody would be the wiser.''

"Right.''

"But somebody was," Clint said, "and they told you about it.''

"Right again," Roper said. "There was a man in the game who didn't appreciate being cheated. He's been waiting for the chance to queer the deal for Belmont and Calhoun, and I gave it to him—and now I'm giving it to you. Use this information to finish Calhoun and Belmont.''

"I can use it against Calhoun, but Belmont's got family money behind him," Clint said. "How do I beat that?''

"You don't," Roper said. "You can put Calhoun out of business and end Charlie Three's little sideline, but you're not going to put an end to Charlie altogether. Just forget about that.''

"Seems to me the whole ambush thing was Charlie's idea."

"So?"

"I wouldn't want to let him get away with that."

"Clint," Roper said, "take what you can get, don't try to go for too much. That's my advice, for what it's worth."

"It's worth a lot," Clint said. "Thanks, Tal."

"I've got to go," Roper said, "but I'll be around. Call on me again if you need to."

"Thanks," Clint said again, and the two men shook hands.

Walking out of the hotel dining room, Roper passed Detective Mike Rucker, who looked as if he was going to say something but didn't.

"Was that—" he started to ask when he reached Clint's table.

"It was," Clint said, "Talbot Roper."

"Oh, geez," Rucker said, sitting down heavily in the seat just vacated by Roper. "A few minutes earlier and I woulda got to meet him."

"Let's get you a beer," Clint said, "and I'll tell you what he had to say."

Rucker looked at Clint.

"Do I need a beer to hear it?"

"No, but you look thirsty."

"I am."

"Wait here," Clint said, standing up. "I'll be back, and then I'll tell you a story about Denver One and Charlie Three."

THIRTY-SEVEN

"The Belmonts?" Rucker said incredulously.

"Well," Clint said, "Charlie Three, as his family calls him."

"Jesus, Clint," Rucker said, "the Belmonts are the most powerful family in Denver."

"Well," Clint said, "as Roper said, you don't have to go after Charles Belmont the third, you can just continue to go after Calhoun, close him down, and that will be the end of Charlie's sideline."

"Yeah, but he won't like that."

"Do you think his father and grandfather know about his business with Calhoun?"

"Probably not," Rucker said. "They're legitimate bankers."

"Well, then, he won't want them to find out."

"What's that mean?"

"It means if you close Calhoun down and put Belmont out of business he's not going to come after you with the full force of his family's name."

"No, I guess he wouldn't."

"It's your call," Clint said. "You're the law, I'm not."

"What would you do?"

"I'd go after both of them," Clint said.

"Why?"

"Because after a reasonable amount of time," Clint said, "Belmont will probably find himself another front man and start all over again, with either the same business or one just as crooked."

"You know," Rucker said, "I won't have any official backing on this."

"Like I said," Clint responded, "it's up to you. Give it some thought. Nobody says you have to make up your mind tonight."

"Yeah."

"Finish your beer," Clint said, and Rucker did. "You done with all your inspector's little jobs?"

"Yeah."

"Then go home, Mike, and decide what you want to do. Whatever it is, I'll back your play."

"I appreciate that, Clint."

Rucker pushed his chair back and got up slowly. He was already thinking about it.

"Don't walk the streets like that, Mike."

"Like what?"

"In a daze," Clint said. "Wait until you get home and then give it some serious thought."

"Yeah," Rucker said, "sure. I'll see you tomorrow."

"Same place for breakfast," Clint said. "You can tell me then what you've decided."

Rucker nodded, waved, and left. Clint wondered what the young man would decide now that he knew he was up against a member of the most powerful banking family in Denver.

THIRTY-EIGHT

As Dancer had requested, Calhoun sent the man a note at his hotel asking him to meet him away from his home. When Calhoun arrived at the Bucket of Blood Saloon, a few blocks from Dancer's hotel—on the "good" side—Dancer was already seated at a table with a bottle of whiskey. Calhoun stopped at the bar, got a mug of beer, and carried it to the table.

"Thanks for meeting me, Johnny," he said.

"You got work for us?"

"I have work for you."

"Just me?"

"That's right."

Johnny Dancer stared at Calhoun with red-rimmed eyes. Calhoun noticed that the level of the whiskey bottle was about halfway.

"Johnny, I need you to do a job for me. I'll pay you the same as I always pay you, but you won't have to split it three ways. This is just for you."

"What is it, Calhoun?"

"I want you to kill the Gunsmith."

"I already told you," Dancer said, "I ain't gonna shoot Adams in the back—"

"You can do it any way you want," Calhoun said, "as long as it gets done."

Dancer considered the request for a few moments, taking the level of the whiskey bottle down another notch. Calhoun nervously sipped at his beer.

"You must really be afraid of him."

"Who wouldn't be?"

"Me," Dancer said, "I wouldn't be."

"Then you'll do it?"

"I'll do it," Dancer said, "for triple the money."

"Triple?"

"This is my last job for you, Calhoun," Dancer said. "No more after this, so it has to pay a lot."

"Yeah, but triple . . ."

"Talk to your partner," Dancer said, "see what he has to say."

"W-who says I have a partner?"

"You're not smart enough to run this yourself, Calhoun. We both know that."

"I don't need to check with nobody," Calhoun said. "I'll pay you triple."

"When do you want it done?"

"As soon as possible," Calhoun said. Then he got brave and added, "As soon as you sober up."

"Oh, don't worry," Dancer said, "I'll sober up."

"Yeah, well," Calhoun said, standing, "let me know when it's done."

"Not so fast."

"What?"

"It'll be done after you pay me."

"After I pay you?" Calhoun said. "You always do the job first, and then get paid."

"This is a different kind of job, isn't it?"

"Dancer—"

"You want it done?" Dancer asked. "Or do you want the Gunsmith to come for you?"

"No, no," Calhoun said, "I want it done. All right, I'll pay you first."

"Get the money and then contact me," Dancer said. "We'll meet then."

"All right," Calhoun said. He looked at his watch. "I have to go."

"Important appointment?"

"Yes," Calhoun said, "very."

He was going to meet with Burke.

"I want double," Burke said.

"You've got it," Calhoun said. "Do you want to be paid first?"

"No, that's okay," Burke said. "I trust you. Just don't tell the others."

"Don't worry," Calhoun said, "this is just between you and me."

THIRTY-NINE

Clint went back to his room and was actually glad that there wasn't a woman waiting for him in bed. Amy and Nina had taken a lot out of him the past couple of days, and he needed a good night's rest.

In the morning he came down and walked to the restaurant where he was to meet Rucker for breakfast. The detective was right, all they seemed to be doing was meeting in restaurants or bars. It was no wonder he was getting frustrated. However, now they knew more then they had ever known before, and Rucker had a big decision to make, one that would affect not only his career, but his life, as well. If he chose to go after Charles Belmont III—Charlie Three—he would probably encounter all sorts of resistance. And if his inspector found out, then he might lose his job before he could accomplish anything.

Clint was drinking his second cup of coffee when Rucker appeared. He walked in and approached the table as if it represented his last meal.

"You look awful."

"Thanks," Rucker said, sitting down. "I didn't get much sleep last night."

"Have you decided?" Clint asked.

The younger man nodded.

"I'm going after them," he said. "All I have to do is figure out how."

"Maybe we can figure it out together."

"I'll also have to figure out what to do for a living if I fail."

"There are a lot of things a smart man can do," Clint said.

"But I've never wanted to be anything but a lawman, Clint."

"You can be a lawman anywhere, Mike," Clint said. "It doesn't have to be Denver."

"This is where I was born and raised," Rucker said. "This is where I wanted to uphold the law."

"Then back off—"

"No," Rucker said, "I can't do that. Once I start doing that, where will it end?"

"Well," Clint said, "right now we only need to concentrate on what to have for breakfast."

"The condemned man ate a hearty meal," Rucker said. "Well, I might as well do that."

When the waiter came to their table, Rucker ordered steak and eggs, and Clint did the same.

After they finished eating they worked on another pot of coffee and discussed their options.

"I thought we could start with Calhoun's men,"

Rucker said. "Take away his men and he has no business."

"He could replace them."

"That would take time."

"How would you go about getting rid of them?"

"Give them a choice," Rucker said. "Leave, or go to jail."

"You'd be bluffing."

Rucker shrugged and said, "Maybe they'll believe the bluff."

"You'll have two problems."

"I know," Rucker said. "Dancer and Burke."

"Dancer won't buy the bluff," Clint said. "If you want him to leave Denver you're going to have to make him."

"And Burke?"

"From what I know of Burke, he's not as smart as Dancer," Clint said, "but he's also not as depressed. He actually likes what he's doing, and the money he's making doing it."

"Then what do you suggest?"

"Work on the lesser men first, and work your way up to Burke and Dancer."

"Then that's what I'll do."

"You're going to need help on this, Mike."

"I have help."

"No," Clint said, shaking his head, "I mean more than just me, and more than your other resources. You're going to have to find out what other policemen are honest and invite them to join you."

Rucker frowned.

"Right now," he said, "I can think of five or six men I could approach."

"You're going to have to be very careful about this," Clint cautioned. "Approach the wrong man and he could give you up to someone like your Inspector Jameson."

"I'll be careful," Rucker said. "I'll pick very carefully."

"That should take you a few days," Clint said. "During that time you can come up with a plan. Once you have your men, they'll have some ideas, too."

"Will you still help?"

"I have no official standing," Clint said, "but I'll do what I can."

"It would be so much easier," Rucker said, "if we could just go in and . . ."

"Kill Calhoun?" Clint asked. "Or Belmont? Maybe we could even ambush them."

"Okay, I know, I know," Rucker said, "that would make us just like them. Why is it they get to act without rules and we don't?"

"That's not a question I can answer," Clint said. "I'm just not that wise."

FORTY

Clint went to Talbot Roper's office for two reasons. One was to let his friend know what was going on. The second reason was to see if Amy was still speaking to him.

"Well, look who it is," Amy said as he entered.

"I can explain."

"I thought you'd run out on me," she said, leaning her elbows on the desk. "I thought I'd scared the great Gunsmith out of Denver."

"I had to change hotels and I had no way of letting you know," Clint said. "I couldn't tell Roper to tell you, because you don't want him to know about us, and you never did tell me where you live."

"And just why did you have to change hotels so abruptly?"

"It was just . . . safer."

"Safer? Safe from what?"

"There are some men in town . . . I'm trying to help this policeman I know . . . look, I really can't get into it that deeply. I just wanted to apologize and let you know that I was still here. I was hoping you'd still be speaking to me.''

She stared at him for a few seconds, then relented and said, ''Oh, I suppose I still am.''

''I'm at a hotel called the Roberts,'' he said, and gave her the location.

''Can I see you tonight?'' she asked.

''I don't see why not,'' he said. It would take Rucker a few days to put his force together. There was no harm in spending his nights with Amy—that is, unless Nina showed up, too.

''Is he in?''

''Yes,'' she said, ''I'll tell him you're here. Come on.''

She knocked on the door, opened it, and said, ''Clint Adams is here, sir.''

''Clint! Come on in.''

Clint and Amy exchanged a smile and then he sidled past her into the room. This time when her breasts pressed against him it was no accident.

''I'm glad you stopped by,'' Roper said. ''I was wondering what you and your young detective had decided to do.''

''Well,'' Clint said, ''he's decided to go after Calhoun and, indirectly, Belmont.''

''Indirectly?''

Clint related to Roper the conversation he and Rucker had had over breakfast.

''So he thinks he's going to take on the Belmont family, huh?''

"Maybe not," Clint said. "Maybe just Charlie Three."

Roper shook his head.

"There's no way you can go after Charlie Three and not have to deal with One and Two. It's just not going to happen that way."

"Unless Charlie Three makes sure it does," Clint said. "He may not want One and Two to know what he's been up to."

"Well, there's your answer then."

"What is?"

"Tell them."

That had never occurred to Clint.

"Just get yourself an appointment with one of them—either you or the detective—march in there and tell them what their son—or grandson—has been up to. One of two things will happen."

"What?"

"Either they won't believe you and they'll have you thrown out . . ."

"Or?"

". . . or they'll put a stop to it, and with no bloodshed."

"You think so?"

"It's just a suggestion, Clint," Roper said. "I really don't know how they'd react to the news. Maybe they'd applaud the lad for his initiative."

"They wouldn't."

"Who knows?"

"But he's trading in murder."

"And how many bodies did they have to climb

over to get where they are today, huh?''

"You've dealt with these people before, Tal,'' Clint said, ''or people just like them. What would their first reaction be?''

"That's easy,'' Roper said. ''To protect the family name. Now, how they would go about that is any-body's guess.''

"Hmm,'' Clint said, ''I guess this is something I'll have to approach Detective Rucker with.''

"Why are you going out of your way to help this young man, if you don't mind my asking?''

"I'm not sure I know the answer to that,'' Clint said. ''Initially, it was because Calhoun was involved, and because I wanted to find out who had taken those shots at me. I think now I just admire him. He's trying to do the right thing in the face of tremendous odds. He can't completely trust his own people, and now he's got the biggest banking family in Denver to deal with—and still he's pressing on.''

"David and Goliath,'' Roper said.

"And David won that one.''

"In this case,'' Roper said, ''I think I'd put my money on the giant.''

"Well,'' Clint said, ''I guess I'm investing more than just my money.''

FORTY-ONE

When Clint came out of Roper's office Amy handed him a piece of paper with something written on it.

"What's this?" he asked.

"My address," she said, "in case you need to switch hotels again."

He smiled, folded it, and put it in his pocket. Then he leaned over and gave her a quick kiss before leaving.

Outside Roper's office Harry Burke stood looking in the window. He saw Clint kiss Amy, smiled, and walked across the street to wait.

He didn't know what hotel Clint Adams was staying at, but he knew that he was friends with Talbot Roper, and that eventually he'd show up at the private investigator's office. He'd simply waited across the street until Clint arrived, and then he'd gone across to take a look in the window.

"You're gonna be easy, Gunsmith," he said.

•   •   •

Inside Amy said, "I also put my last name on there."

"Which is?"

"Manning."

"Hello, Amy Manning."

"Clint, do you know how much longer you'll be in Denver?"

"Probably at least a week, until I see this . . . thing through."

"And then where will you go?"

"I'm not sure," he said. "I was headed down to Texas when I came through. I expect I'll just continue on that way."

"Well," she said, "since I intend to be working here for a very long time I guess I'll see you whenever you come back to Denver."

"I expect you will, Amy, but for now why don't we take it one day at a time?"

"All right," she said, "starting with tonight."

"I'll even tell the desk clerk to let you into my room," he said, "so you won't have to charm him into it."

He kissed her again, shortly, then left.

Across the street Burke saw Clint leave the office. He could have shot him from there, but Harry Burke knew he wasn't the best shot with a handgun, and if he missed he'd be in trouble. No, he had to plan this out carefully so there'd be no mistakes.

He didn't bother following Clint because he didn't think he could get away with that. Better to follow the girl when she came out. Sooner or later, she'd lead him to Clint Adams's hotel.

Clint walked down the street, away from Talbot Roper's office, totally unaware of the man across the street. If Burke had stepped out of his doorway and tried to follow Clint, then he would have noticed him. This way, however, there was really nothing to notice.

Johnny Dancer had collected his money from Lyle Calhoun earlier that morning. He stood in the doorway on the same side as Talbot Roper's office. He had to hand it to Burke, the man had the same idea he did.

It didn't surprise Dancer to see Burke, and didn't surprise him that Calhoun had sent both him and Burke after Clint Adams at the same time. Calhoun was a double-dealer from way back. He doubted, however, that Burke had collected his money up front. Calhoun's moneyman was apparently rich enough, though, to pay Dancer his three-times the normal fee, and not worry about losing it for nothing if Burke was the one who got Clint Adams.

Only Burke wasn't going to be the one that got him. Johnny Dancer was going to see to that.

FORTY-TWO

Clint was starting to wish he could do what Detective Mike Rucker was thinking of doing that very morning. If he could walk into Calhoun's house and just kill him . . . but that wouldn't solve anything. Oh, it would square his beef with Calhoun, but Belmont would probably go on—as Clint had told Rucker at breakfast—with a different front man.

Clint had to get his own priorities straight. Did he just want to find out who shot at him and get rid of Calhoun, or go all the way and somehow get to Charlie Three?

Oh, just maybe he wanted to do all three.

When he got to his new hotel he found his new friend, Spike, waiting for him in the lobby.

"Hello, Spike. What brings you here?"

"Thought you might need some help."

"Doing what?"

"Gettin' around," Spike said, "maybe gettin' a

girl—oh, wait, you got a girl, don't ya? In fact, you got two.'' The grin on Spike's face was all Clint needed to convince him that the boy was fifteen, not nine or ten, or even twelve. It was as lascivious a grin as he'd ever seen on a grown man.

"That's right," Clint said, "but I don't think I need any help getting around, either."

"Maybe you wanna send somebody a message?"

"No, I don't think—wait a minute. Maybe I do. In fact, maybe I want to send more than one."

"I'm your man."

"Are you hungry?"

"Hey," Spike said, "I could always eat. I'm still growing, ya know."

Clint hoped so.

"Come on inside and have something to eat while I think about these messages."

"You talked me into it."

Spike went through two lunches by the time Clint had both messages written out with paper and pencil he'd gotten from the front desk.

"Now, you're sure you know where this place is?" Clint asked.

"I know exactly where it is," Spike said. "Nobody knows this city like me, Clint."

"Okay, and you've got the address for this other message?"

"I got it." Spike picked up his third glass of milk and downed it enthusiastically.

"Are you full?"

Spike belched and said, "I can always eat, but I think I've had enough for now."

"Then get going and deliver those messages," Clint said, handing Spike some money.

"Whoa, what's all this?"

"So you can take a cab if your legs get tired."

"Thanks, Clint! If I had more customers like you I'd be rich in a week."

"Just remember to come back and let me know the messages were delivered."

"I'll be back before you know I'm gone."

With that the boy leapt up from his chair and darted out of the room.

"It wasn't something he ate, I hope," the waiter said.

"Nope," Clint assured him, "it was something I said."

Calhoun was sitting in his office, wringing his hands and worrying, when Leo came to the door.

"What?" Calhoun snapped.

"This just came for you, boss."

"What is it?"

"I don't know," Leo said. "I didn't read it."

"Well, who delivered it?"

"A kid."

"Bring it here, then."

Leo crossed the room and handed Calhoun the folded piece of paper. It wasn't even in an envelope. With a longing look at the decanter on the desk, Leo left.

Calhoun unfolded the paper and read the writing on it, then crumpled the message in his hand. He grabbed the gun out of his desk, checked it to make sure it was loaded, and then laid it on top of the desk. There'd be no more keeping it in a drawer. If Burke or Dancer didn't get the job done soon, he might have to get to that gun quick.

Calhoun began to go through his options. If it came to it, if it was Clint Adams or the police who came to him, he could offer them Charlie Three to go easy on him. Wouldn't that police detective just love to take down a member of Denver's biggest banking family?

But Adams, he thought, what would he care? He only wants to kill me.

He was starting to worry about having sent both Dancer and Burke after Clint Adams. What if they got in each other's way? They didn't like each other at all. What if Dancer told Burke that he had been paid triple his regular fee, while Burke was only getting double? And what if he told Burke he'd been paid up front?

Jesus, now he was making himself afraid of Clint Adams, Harry Burke, and Johnny Dancer—and Charlie Three. Calhoun was starting to wonder if it wouldn't have been easier for him to have just stayed a bounty hunter himself.

Naw, he wasn't good at it, not at all, plus he'd hated it—but then he'd hated every job he'd ever had, except this one. In the beginning being a front man for Charlie Three had been great. Plenty of money, access to the girls at Lillian's whenever he wanted, the best food and brandy . . . when had it gone so wrong?

That was easy.

Clint Adams.

As soon as the Gunsmith got to town things had started to turn. Why was Clint Adams always ruining things for him?

He picked the gun up off the desk. He was safe here. If Adams came for him he would have to come through the door, there was no other way in. If Calhoun just stayed in this room, and Burke and Dancer both failed, Clint Adams would have to come through that door . . . and then he'd have him!

He just had to stay right here at his desk.

FORTY-THREE

Amy Manning had no idea that she was being followed to Clint Adams's hotel. In fact, she had no idea she was being followed by two men.

Actually, Burke was following her and Dancer was following Burke, but it amounted to the same thing.

Burke stopped outside as Amy went into the lobby. He crossed the street and took up a position in a doorway from where he had a clear view of the front door.

Dancer didn't need to see the hotel front door, he needed to see Burke, so he took a position in an alley on the same side of the street as the hotel.

Inside Amy presented herself to the desk clerk, who had already been instructed to give her a key to Clint's room.

Burke figured Clint had to either come in or go out, and when he did he'd take him. It'd be dark by then, and Adams wouldn't be expecting it. He'd close the ground between them and take the Gunsmith out with his pistol before the man had a chance to react.

Dancer decided he didn't need to move until Burke did, so he folded his arms and got comfortable.

It would all happen soon.

In point of fact Clint was already in the hotel, he just wasn't in the room. He was in the dining room having a piece of pie and a cup of coffee. He was waiting for Spike to come back and tell him that both messages had been delivered. He figured the boy would be ready for a piece of pie by the time he got back.

He was hoping that the two messages he had sent would cause something to happen. If they did, then Rucker might not even need to put together a small team of policemen. Maybe it would end before then.

It seemed to him he'd been in Denver for weeks, not days, and that most of those days had been spent like this, sitting at a table with a beer or a cup of coffee. Instead of sitting back and waiting for something to happen, it was time to shake things up and make them happen.

He had no idea how close he was right at that moment to having that happen.

Burke decided to get brave and take a look in the lobby. Maybe he could get the room number from the desk clerk. He stepped out of the doorway and was about to cross the street when he saw a boy running toward the hotel. He thought he recognized him as one of the street urchins who did odd jobs for two bits of a dollar. He allowed the boy to go in first, and then crossed the street. He had a hunch, and since the stakes were high he thought he'd play it out.

Dancer was surprised to see Burke moving so soon. He also saw the boy run into the hotel, and he knew who the boy was. His name was Spike, and he ran errands for change. Dancer was thinking what Burke was thinking. If he'd known that it probably would have upset him. He waited for Burke to cross the street, then left his alley and moved toward the front door of the hotel.

Burke entered the lobby and saw the boy going into the dining room. He hurried to the doorway and peered in, saw the boy join Clint Adams at a table.

Burke liked this better, inside rather than outside, and he could use the boy. It also helped that the dining room was empty except for Clint, the boy, and their waiter.

Yes, this was very good, better than he'd expected. All he had to do was wait.

Dancer looked into the lobby and saw Burke, who was looking in a doorway, probably to the dining room. Dancer already knew, by instinct, that everyone was in place. Clint Adams was in the dining room, Burke in the lobby, and he was in position to take them both out, if necessary.

But there was still some waiting to be done.

* * *

"Both messages delivered?" Clint asked Spike.

"Yep."

"You want a piece of pie?"

"Sure."

"What kind?"

"Peach?"

"Comin' up."

"We got time?"

"Why not?"

"Because of the man."

"What man?"

"The man across the street."

Clint stopped waving at the waiter and stared at Spike.

"What man across what street?"

FORTY-FOUR

From the description Spike gave Clint the man had to be Burke. Clint decided to let Burke wait while Spike had his pie.

"You ain't afraid?" Spike asked.

"No."

"Why not?"

"I don't feel the man's any real danger to me."

"Why not? Maybe he wants to shoot you."

"Well, if he tries," Clint said, "I'll shoot him."

"That's all there is to it?"

"That's all."

After the pie Clint waited to settle the bill and said to Spike, "You'd better get on home, Spike."

"You don't need me for anything else?"

"Not today. You've been a big help, though. Thanks."

He handed the boy ten dollars, and his eyes popped as he accepted the money.

"Thanks!"

"Go ahead, now," Clint said. "I'm going to pay my bill and go upstairs."

"You got company, huh?" Spike asked, smiling.

"Get out of here, Spike."

The boy laughed and walked from the dining room into the lobby. Clint figured Burke was still waiting outside for him, only he wasn't going outside.

He gave the waiter the money for the pie and coffee and milk, and walked out to the lobby. As he stepped through the doorway he stopped cold. Burke smiled at him from behind Spike. The man had his left arm around the boy's throat and was holding his gun in his right hand.

"Big surprise, huh, Gunsmith?" Burke asked.

Angry with himself, Clint said, "That's right, Burke. Big surprise."

"Now, you do exactly what I say or I'll kill this boy."

"You're calling it."

Clint tried to keep his eyes right on Burke.

"Take your gun out and drop it onto the floor," Burke said.

"I don't think so, Burke."

"Do it!" Burke snapped. "I'll kill this kid. I will." He just about screwed the barrel of his gun into Spike's ear.

"You just take it easy, Spike," Clint said to the boy.

"I ain't scared, Clint," Spike said.

"Attaboy," Clint said.

"Come on, Adams," Burke said. "What's it gonna be?"

"Just give me a few seconds more, Burke."

"For what?"

The voice behind Burke said, "For me to blow a hole in the back of your head, Burke."

Burke froze, his eyes darting around.

"That you, Dancer?"

"That's right," Dancer said, pressing the barrel of his gun against Burke's spine, "it's me."

"What are you doin' here?"

"Right now I'm about to blow out your spine if you don't let the boy go."

"You're crazy," Burke said. "We're both after the same thing, here."

"Maybe," Dancer said, "but we're going about it very differently. I ain't trying to hide behind a kid. Now let . . . him . . . go!"

Dancer cocked the hammer back on his gun, and Burke released the boy.

"Okay, there!" Burke said.

"Get behind the desk, Spike," Clint said.

Spike ran behind the front desk, where the clerk was crouched.

"Is it over?" the clerk whispered to him.

"Not yet."

"Now what?" Burke asked, holding his hands out to his sides.

"Holster your gun."

"He'll kill me."

"Or maybe you'll kill him," Dancer said. "It'll be a fair fight, Burke."

"I ain't no gunman!"

"No," Dancer said, "just a back-shooter."

"I just did that to try and get in good with Calhoun," Burke said, holstering his gun. He looked at Clint. "You gotta believe me, Adams. It weren't nothin' personal."

"It was you who tried to ambush me?" Clint asked.

"It weren't nothin' personal," Burke said. "We saw you in Box Springs, figured you were headed this way."

"So you got ahead of me and waited."

"It weren't—"

"I'm stepping away now, Burke," Dancer said. "This is between you and Adams."

With that Dancer moved aside, out of the line of fire.

"What's the matter, Burke?" Clint asked. "You afraid to try to kill a man who's facing you?"

"This ain't fair!"

"It's as fair a chance as you'll ever get," Clint said.

"Dancer!" Burke wailed, and then he went for his gun. Clint shot him dead before he cleared leather.

"Wow!" Spike said.

Clint walked to Burke's body and checked it. The man was dead. At the sound of the shot several people came running down from the second floor to see what the commotion was. One of them was Amy.

"What happened?" she demanded.

"Go back upstairs, Amy," Clint said. "Everything's all right." He looked at Spike. "Spike, go and get a policeman."

"Right!" The boy ran out the door.

Clint looked over at Dancer.

"Thanks."

"I just didn't want him doing what I was already paid to do."

"Dancer—"

"Holster it, Adams," Dancer said. "It's my turn."

FORTY-FIVE

"Do you really want to do this, Dancer?" Clint asked.

"I don't have a choice."

"I don't understand. Why stop Burke? Why save the boy? I don't get it."

"You deserve a fair chance, Adams," Dancer said. "I couldn't see you being killed by a coward hiding behind a little boy."

"So you saved me just so you could kill me?"

"Calhoun paid me a lot of money to kill you."

"Did he pay you enough to die?"

"I don't know," Dancer said. "I guess I'll find out soon enough."

"And what if I don't oblige you?"

"Then I'll kill you," Dancer said, "and I'll do it standing in front of you, not from behind some rock or tree."

"And will that make up for those you already killed that way?"

Dancer hesitated a moment, then said, "No, it won't. Nothing will make up for that."

Clint looked over at the stairs. All the spectators had gone back to their rooms except for Amy.

"Wait until I get the girl to go back to the room, Dancer."

"Go ahead and do it, then."

Clint walked to the stairs, stayed on the first floor while Amy was halfway up.

"Amy, go back to the room."

"Why? So I can hear a shot and wonder if it's you who's dead?"

"You're better off up there."

"I want to stay."

He looked at Dancer, then back at Amy and lowered his voice.

"I might get killed because I'm worried about you," he said. "If you go up I can concentrate on what I'm doing."

"But, Clint—"

"Now go, Amy. Go!"

She bit her lip, then turned and went up the stairs. Clint turned and faced Dancer.

"Thanks, Dancer."

"I'm not looking for anyone else to get hurt, Adams," Dancer said. "I'm just doing what I was paid to do."

"Well, then, do it," Clint said. "Let's get it over with. I've got somebody waiting for me in my room."

"You're pretty confident, huh?"

"I've been doing this for a lot of years, Dancer," Clint said. "It's gotten so I pretty much know when I can take somebody, and I can take you."

"You think so?"

"I'm telling you so. You have a chance to change your mind, turn around, and walk out."

"Can't do it."

"Think about it," Clint said. "You don't want to end up like him."

"You're forgetting something."

"What's that?"

"I just saw your move, and I wasn't impressed," Dancer said. "You haven't seen mine."

Clint grinned.

"My move is only as good as it has to be, Dancer," he said. "Burke was right, he was no gunman. He was slow."

"I'm not."

"I don't doubt it."

"It's time to stop talking."

Clint shrugged and said, "Whenever you're ready."

At that moment Spike appeared at the front door, and Clint was surprised to see Rucker with him. He hadn't expected the boy to come back with *that* policeman.

"Clint," the detective said.

"Stay back, Mike," Clint said. "It seems like it's got to be this way."

"But . . . I can't let this happen."

"You don't have a choice, policeman," Dancer said, and went for his gun.

Both Spike and Rucker blinked, and before the blink was completed, Johnny Dancer was dead.

FORTY-SIX

The cab pulled up in front of Calhoun's house and Charles Belmont III stared at it. His money had paid for this place. How dare Calhoun send him a message threatening to expose him if he didn't come to his house to see him. Incensed, Charlie Three had stewed in his office awhile, wondering how to handle it. He finally decided he'd go and see Calhoun, just as the man demanded, and while he was there he would end the relationship and take the house right out from under the man. He'd put him on the street, where he belonged.

He got out of the cab and walked to the front door. He pounded on the door and it was answered by Leo.

"Mr. Belmont, sir," Leo said.

"Hello, Leo. Where is he?"

"In the office, sir, but—"

"I know the way," Belmont said. "You'd better pack his things, Leo. Calhoun is leaving."

"Yes, sir," Leo said happily. After all, he worked

in the house with Calhoun, but he was paid by Belmont. And if Calhoun was out, that meant there was a spot open at the top.

Leo ran upstairs to pack.

Calhoun heard the knock at the door, heard the voices, and his hand tightened on the gun. He couldn't make out what was being said, but then he heard a man yell, "Calhoun! Damn you!"

Since he'd been waiting for Clint Adams to come and get him, that's whose voice he imagined he heard. As the man appeared in the doorway he lifted the gun from the desk, aimed, and fired once.

The next time Leo opened the front door it was to admit Clint and Rucker.

"Who are you?" Leo demanded.

"Detective Rucker. Where's Calhoun?"

"In the office, but . . . something terrible's happened."

"Take us there."

Leo shrugged. What else was there to do?

He showed them to the office, and as Clint and Rucker entered they saw the body on the floor. Rucker immediately produced his gun and pointed it at Calhoun, who was still seated behind his desk.

"Drop your gun, Calhoun!"

Calhoun looked up, saw Rucker and Clint.

"You bastard!" he said to Clint. "I thought he was you. You set us up."

"Calhoun—" Rucker shouted, but the man didn't

listen. He lifted his gun again, and Rucker shot him. The bullet struck him in the chest and drove him back in his chair. The gun fell from his nerveless fingers and clattered to the floor.

"Jesus," Rucker said, looking down at the body, "it's Charlie Three."

"So it is," Clint said. He'd had his hand on his gun, ready in case Rucker faltered.

The detective turned to Clint.

"What did he mean, you set him up?"

"I had Spike deliver two messages," Clint said. "I thought they'd make something happen."

"What messages?"

"The one to Calhoun said I was coming for him," Clint answered. "The one to Charlie Three I wrote as if from Calhoun, threatening to expose him if he didn't come here."

"He was right, then," Rucker said. "You did set them up. When Belmont came through the door, Calhoun panicked and shot him, thinking it was you coming to get him."

"Like I said," Clint responded. "I was just trying to make something happen."

"Well," Rucker said, "I guess you did that."

Watch for

THE JAMES BOYS

200th novel in the exciting GUNSMITH series
from Jove

Coming in September!

JAKE LOGAN

TODAY'S HOTTEST ACTION WESTERN!